# Revenge

## Yacht Kings
### Book 1

## Renee Rose

# Want FREE Renee Rose books?

also get bonus epilogues, special pricing, exclusive previews and news of new releases.

# Prologue

**D**ahlia

One more dance with a spoiled, cocky teen in a tux and I'm going to poke my eye out with a cocktail toothpick.

I reach out and grab one of said toothpicks from a waiter's tray, the one presently attached to a cashew-crusted salmon bite, and pop the food in my mouth. I'm hoping to forestall any more conversation with my current suitor, Archie, a Manhattan blueblood whose father works at one of the white shoe law firms on Wall Street.

"I like your necklace." His gaze is not at the seven-figure diamond arrangement on my neck, but at the cleavage showing above the strapless bodice of my gown. At least he's attracted to some part of the real me, even if it's just my body.

We're on my father's newest and biggest yacht, *Debutante*, built specifically for my coming-of-age ball. Naturally, my mother needed the most pretentious place possible, so she can show off the Yacht King's immeasurable wealth and status. It's important to outdo every other society family in New York.

Frankly, I don't see the point of having a coming-out party when it's not like I will actually get to date. I won't actually choose my own husband. I won't be giving my precious virginity to someone who steals my heart, makes me tremble, and kisses me like his life depends on it.

Nope.

My marriage has pretty much already been arranged.

I'm going to be a president's wife.

A first lady.

That's what Babs, my ambitious mother, believes, anyway. That's the future she wants for me. For her. For our family.

Across the dance floor, my intended—eighteen-year-old Jake Reese the Third, Senator Jacob Reese's son—holds court with a group of young socialites who moon over every gilded word he utters.

We shared a first dance, during which he looked down his nose and told me I'm still far too young for him to associate with, and we haven't spoken since.

Which suits me just fine. I only have one real friend here, and that's Bea, but she's presently occupied on the dance floor with a flat-footed cousin of mine.

"Would you care to dance?" Henrik, some kind of Norwegian prince, bows and offers his hand.

Archie, knowing he's outranked, politely moves away.

Henrik is sweet. I've met him before on visits to our Norwegian shipyard. He's good-looking and polite. But my feet are killing me in these heels, and I'm tired of making forced conversation, smiling, and being on display.

Unfortunately, my mother's eagle eyed me every minute of this excruciating event. I glance over at her.

She has her back to me at the moment, talking to Loretta Reese, the senator's wife.

Now is my chance.

"I would love to, but I need to take a quick break. Excuse me while I go to the powder room?" Using a question allows him to be the hero.

"Of course." Henrik inclines his golden head politely. His perfect manners match his perfect blond hair and flawless accent.

"Thank you. I will find you when I return," I promise, sailing away as fast as my high heels will allow.

I head toward the restroom in case my mom is looking then quickly detour down the stairs to the kitchen.

I get a few surprised looks as I dash through the galley and come out on the narrow servants' deck. Several servers who were standing around gabbing snap to attention.

One doesn't move at all, except to eye me as he takes a slow drag on a cigarette while leaning against the rail of the deck.

*Oh, damn.*

He has dark hair that curls over one side of his forehead and a *I don't give two fucks* attitude. Dressed in the crisp white shirt, black pants, bowtie, and cumberbund of the hired waiters, he somehow manages to look more regal than any prince, Norwegian or otherwise.

He takes in the fluffy meringue of my pale pink strapless gown, the elbow-length calfskin gloves, and the necklace worth more than my college fund with a bored look.

My body heats at his perusal.

My first thought is that he doesn't know who I am. He can't possibly understand that this is my father's yacht, and the way he's looking at me would be considered impertinent.

Then I realize he *must* know I'm somebody.

And he really doesn't care.

On the contrary, his derisive look seems to imply *I'm* interrupting *him* at this moment. That this is his territory, and I'm the intruder.

My pulse picks up speed. Maybe that's the appeal. He's obviously the bad boy who doesn't follow the rules. James Dean and Elvis rolled into one delicious package.

He surely must comprehend I could have him fired in a heartbeat.

I stride over and lean a hip against the rail beside him. He's even more good-looking up close. His eyes are the shade of whiskey, and his lashes are thick and long for a man.

"Give me a drag," I demand.

He arches a dark brow. It's a sexy look on him. Almost swoon-worthy. I don't breathe during the four interminable seconds it takes him to react, but eventually, he turns the cigarette around and holds it to my lips.

There's something intimate about the action. He doesn't hand it to me–he controls the way it comes to my mouth. When it leaves. I smell the clean soap of his washed hands, along with the tobacco and ash.

I've never smoked before in my life.

I realize, belatedly, that this is a terrible idea. The scent will be all over me–in my gown. On my breath.

I'm supposed to return to the deck dance floor to be the society darling of the night, and I'm making a faux pas that could cause every woman in my mother's circle to cluck their tongue. *Smoking!*

But the handsome waiter's looking at me with a challenge in his shrewd gaze. I realize he sees it all–my naivete, my foolish rebellion.

4

I don't think he's amused, either. He's not finding me cute. In fact, there's a note of scorn behind those dark eyes.

So I rise to the challenge. I close my pink-lipsticked mouth around the butt of his cigarette and suck.

And choke.

Cough.

Try to drag fresh air in to cool my heated throat and lungs.

Cough some more.

When I steal a look at the stranger's face, I find him still regarding me coolly.

He takes another slow drag of the cigarette, watching me the entire time. He turns his head to blow the smoke away from my face but doesn't break eye contact.

"This your ball?"

The fist that's been in my solar plexus since the moment I woke up and my mother started berating me about everything I had to do, everything that wasn't perfect about me yet, tightens. I stare past him into the inky black of the water below. "Supposedly."

He catches the bitterness of my tone, and the corners of his lips turn up. The resulting smile is devastating. My knees weaken, and heat swirls in my core.

"So you're back here rebelling?" His grin grows. It transforms his face, giving him a more open, boyish look.

I take the cigarette from his fingers and attempt another drag. Cough some more. "I guess."

"Well." He gives me a sweeping, critical gaze. "You wear it well."

I lift a surprised gaze to his face, trying to gauge if he means it. I wasn't expecting a compliment. I thought for sure he'd throw derision.

Once I look, I find it impossible to look away. I'm

blasted by his good looks. The crinkles at the corners of his eyes, a Roman nose, and a square jaw. Large hands that look like they could inflict great damage.

*Or pleasure...*

He takes the cigarette from my fingers and tosses it into the water. "Well, then." He holds out his palm like a gentleman.

I'm suddenly dizzy as I contemplate taking it. As if I know, somehow, that if I do, my life will never be the same.

"Come on." He tips his head away from the rail like he has some plan. "Let's see if we can get you into some real trouble."

# Chapter One

*1964 (7 years later), Newport, RI*

**A**ntonio

"Your time is up." Clad in a tuxedo tailored to fit my broad-shouldered frame, I lean against the brownstone church wall of St. Mary's Cathedral. There's no gun in my hand. I don't need one.

Benedict King knows me. He knows why I'm here. That I represent the don of the Beretta family. He probably also sees I have men stationed everywhere around the churchyard, mingling with the eight hundred guests streaming in for the society wedding of the season.

"Please, *please*." The man holds up plump, shaking hands. Sweat drips from his hairline. "It's my daughter's wedding. Just let me walk down the aisle with her. Please allow me to get her married before you kill me."

My upper lip curls at the mention of his precious daughter. "Who says I'm not here to kill her, too?" I ask casually.

Terror flares in the fat man's eyes. He blinks rapidly, his

pupils tiny pricks of black in his pale blue eyes. He's in a white tux, as if *he's* the virgin being sold off in matrimony today, rather than his spoiled daughter.

"Don't touch Dahlia." Spittle flies from his mouth.

"The moment you fucked the Berettas, your life, your wife's life, and your daughter's were forfeit. And I'm here to collect."

A bead of sweat rolls down his forehead. "You can't–"

"Benedict! Where have you been? The ceremony's about to start!" Barbara King–or Babs, as the society column calls her–comes rushing around the corner then stops short when she sees me. One look at her husband, and she realizes things are not right. "Who are you? What's going on?"

I give her a shark tooth grin. "I'm the guy who's come to kill you, Babs."

She sways on her feet, color draining from her face.

"Catch her before she faints," I tell her asswipe husband.

Benedict's reflexes are slow, but he does manage to grab his wife's elbow before she topples.

"Benedict," she sobs. "What's happening? What did you do?" She searches his face.

He stares back at her, his expression conveying his dismay. His regret. The horror of what's about to happen. "The money I lost in the Shellingham deal, Babs. It was borrowed." He glances at me.

Babs turns a slow, terrified gaze on me. "From *the mafia?*" she croaks.

"That's right, doll," I say. "And the Yacht King missed his window to make it right with Don Beretta. So it's not going to be the happily-ever-after you had planned for your beautiful Dahlia today."

Just saying the girl's name makes my upper lip curl with

disgust. The girl I shouldn't have touched all those years ago.

But this is the day I finally get my revenge.

Make the Yacht King and his precious debutante pay.

He doesn't remember me. Why would he? I was just the guy he pinned as the *blue-collar brute* in a monkey suit at his daughter's coming out ball. Probably one of a thousand guys whose lives he's ruined.

"Wait! Isn't there anything we can do?" Babs begs. "The yachts? Benedict, give him the inventory! It must be worth a fortune!"

I fold my arms across my chest to show I'm listening. I didn't actually come here to kill them, not that I won't if I have to. But dead bodies don't make the don rich, so I'm really here to take everything the Yacht King owns.

Including his prize daughter.

Except she's not for the don.

She's for me.

Benedict darts a nervous look at his wife. "Y-yes. I can give you the inventory. Forty-five yachts in various stages of build."

Forty-five yachts that have all been purchased already. The once-wealthy ship-builder is up to his ears in debt. But sure, the don would take the inventory and leave Benedict to answer to his other creditors.

That's what he sent me here to do.

I want more, though.

I didn't come here for a piece of his pie.

I came to take his whole world.

To demolish this worm of a man.

The don won't be happy, but I'll fix that later. I will run the business for him and give him the proceeds. Make him rich with a legitimate business. Besides, once I explain to him the significant advantages to having our own sea vessels out on the water for smuggling arms and other contraband, he will crown me Prince of the Beretta family.

I say nothing.

"Take the houses. The cars! Anything!" Babs begs. "Please, just tell us what to do, and we'll do it."

Ah. That's exactly the opening I was looking for.

"I'll take the business. King Yacht Company."

Benedict looks like he's going to be sick, but his wife exclaims, "Yes!" almost before the words are out of my mouth. I take a sheaf of folded papers from the inner pocket of my tuxedo jacket.

"Sign over everything you own to me," I command.

"Do it!" Babs exclaims.

"Fine. Give me a pen," Benedict snaps.

I wait until he's signed every line before I deliver the final blow. "This almost takes care of your debt."

Babs goes bug-eyed. "What else do you want?" Her voice is practically a screech.

"I'll take your daughter."

That statement makes them both freeze. They stare at me with obvious horror.

"Wh-what do-oo you mean our daughter?" Babs' chin wobbles.

I spread my hands. "You planned a wedding. The event of the season. We'll make it official. Your daughter marries me today to seal the deal. That way, it will all make sense. The business was turned over to your new son-in-law."

"No!" Babs is horrified.

Benedict staggers to the right and clutches at his chest.

"I'll keep her safe so long as you maintain your end of the bargain."

Now Benedict understands me. There will be no going

to the police. No trying to reverse this deal. No using his connections with Senator Reese or his limp-dick mayor son to bring down the Beretta crime family.

No, he must marry into *La Famiglia* if he wants to live and if he wants me to treat his daughter like the shining pearl he and Babs believe the spoiled socialite to be.

He gives a jerky nod. "Okay."

"What?" Babs crumples, her knees giving way again. Her husband has to hold her up. "You can't," she croaks. "Benedict...the wedding."

"*My* wedding," I say. "My wedding to the girl you once told me I wasn't worthy of. *Not even to lick the shit off her designer heels.*" I lift my brows at Benedict. I envisioned this moment every day I was in prison on trumped-up charges put there by this man. "Do you remember that?"

Benedict blinks in confusion, his mouth open.

No, he doesn't remember. He's fucked too many of those he considers lower class to count.

"At her coming out ball. Surely you recall. The *blue-collar brute?*"

I watch as the flush of recognition then rage transforms his expression. "*You.*"

I nod. "Me."

He throws an arm wide. "*This?* That's what this is about?"

I could not put more satisfaction into a smile. Yes. All of this. Seven years in the making. From becoming my uncle's right-hand man after prison to orchestrating all of Benedict King's failed investments and making sure he took the cash loan he could never pay back.

Yes, I've been directing the downfall of Benedict King since that night of the ball when his security guards beat me to a pulp and then dragged me to the police station with lies that no one should have believed.

And today is deliverance.

I now own Benedict King, his wife, and most importantly, that stuck-up virgin of his.

The one who is about to swear to love, honor, and obey me.

\* \* \*

*Dahlia*

There's a tiara on my head. I wanted a wreath of flowers. The kind with ribbons that fall down the back to mingle with soft curls, but my mother wouldn't have it.

My hair's in an up-do to display the diamond engagement earrings Jake gave me at our engagement party. I argued that the tiara actually detracts from the earrings, but in the end, I had no say in the matter.

It may be my wedding, but like every other moment in my life, it belongs to my parents.

Bea, my best friend—the one who I wanted to be my Maid of Honor, but my mother nixed—brushes a little more rouge on my cheeks.

"You look pale. You're not going to puke, are you?"

I stare out the church window at the guests streaming in. Hundreds of people I don't really know.

Of course, I've memorized all their names and stations. I know who is who and what they mean to both my family and the Reeses. I know I have to schmooze every single one of them today.

That's my job.

This wedding isn't about marriage at all. It's a political event planned by the Reeses and my parents to boost Jake's

Mayoral career and get him to the governorship of New York City.

This will be my job for the rest of my life: looking beautiful, remembering names. Charming the right people.

"If I do, there won't be much to puke. I haven't eaten anything today."

"Well, maybe that's the problem," Bea clucks. "I'll go and get you something."

The door to the room opens, and my mom pokes her head in. "It's time. Come here, Dahlia. There's been a change of plans."

There's a wild, hysterical look about my mom. For once, she's not giving me the critical once-over to tell me everything that's not perfect about me at the moment. Something must've gone wrong downstairs.

The priest didn't arrive. Or Jake's sister, my bitchy maid of honor, sprained her ankle or something. Whatever it is, at least she can't pin it on me.

"Bea, leave us for a minute," my mom commands.

"Of course, Mrs. King. I was about to go find something for Dahlia to eat." Bea rolls her eyes at me as she passes behind my mom's back and blows me a kiss.

I know something's really wrong when my mom doesn't tell Bea I can't eat because my stomach will pooch in the wedding dress.

"Listen to me, Dahlia." My mom grabs my bare shoulders and squeezes so hard I try to pull away. She shakes me.

"Mom, you're going to leave marks!" I exclaim. I can't imagine she'd want her precious daughter's snowy-white shoulders to have red blotches when she walks down the aisle.

*"Listen to me."*

Something about her tone startles me out of my irritability. I've never heard her speak this way. She's always so controlled and ladylike. Even when she's throwing daggers.

I go still. "What is it? Is it Daddy?"

My dad is overweight and stressed. Total heart attack material.

"No. Yes. Listen!"

My voice raises in pitch. "I'm listening, Mom. *Tell me what's going on.*"

"You're going to walk down that aisle, and you're going to marry the man at the altar."

I blink. *Well, obviously.*

Has my mother taken too much Valium?

"And?"

My mother shakes her head urgently.

Clearly, there's something I'm not understanding.

Bea knocks on the door and pops her head in. "You two, it's time! Everyone's waiting."

"You'll marry the man at the altar," my mom repeats, as if those words hold deep meaning.

"That's the plan," I say with false brightness. Jake Reese, my intended from the time I was thirteen years old.

A man I neither love nor even really admire. He's a pompous ass who only cares about himself.

I flash a bewildered look at Bea, who holds my giant peach and white rose bouquet out to me.

She shrugs. "Show time." She picks up the train of my gown, so I can walk ahead of her.

"Promise me," my mom calls out behind us. "Promise me you'll do it."

*What in the actual fuck is going on?*

It doesn't matter. I don't have time to deal with her histrionics this afternoon.

"I'm doing it right now, Mom." I don't turn around. We

arrived at the doors to the cathedral nave where the rest of the wedding party waits.

My mom takes the arm of one of the groomsmen. "All of our lives depend on it," she hisses at me just before she enters.

"Jesus H. Christ. Did she get into the liquor cabinet?" Bea whispers.

I smother a laugh. Thank God for Bea, or I'd never make it through this day.

She takes the arm of her groomsman and walks down the aisle.

I don't see Britt, my Maid of Honor. Maybe she already walked? I'm confused.

The flower girl heads down the aisle tossing her rose petals.

"Our turn." My dad holds out his arm.

As I take it, I realize that he, too, looks terrible. I stop. "Dad? What's going on?"

He's sweating. Breathing hard. It looks like he's about to keel over. "Did your mother talk to you?"

"Yes, but I don't understand. What's happening?"

"Just walk down that aisle and say your vows to the man on the other side, and we'll all make it through this day." He tugs me forward into the nave.

Eight hundred bodies stand as the violinists begin Wagner's "Bridal Chorus".

*We'll all make it through this day.*

My feet move forward. The train of my gown swishes behind me. I can't figure out what my dad is saying. None of this makes sense.

The guests turn expectantly my way. I hear murmurings, but they aren't about how lovely I look. There's a buzz of wondering whispers.

*Who is she marrying? Where's Jake? What's going on?*

I widen my pasted smile and look to the end of the aisle at my groom.

That's when I realize that it's not the future mayor of New York City standing at the altar waiting for me.

It's someone else. Someone with dark hair watching me intently.

Now I understand what my parents meant. *I'm marrying someone else today.* And it's life or death.

The air rips from my lungs as I grow closer.

My God.

It can't be.

It's *him. The guy from the ball.*

# Chapter Two

*Antonio*

Dahlia drops her bouquet.

Her lips part.

Benedict stoops to pick up the cascade of roses and hands it to her. "Say your vows," he hisses as he deposits her at the altar and lifts her veil.

Dahlia hasn't looked away from me, her pale blue gaze locked in mine. She whirls to look over her shoulder at her mother, crying in the first pew. Then she scans the exits, no doubt noting I have every one of them covered.

"Nowhere to run, Dahlia," I murmur. "You just got sold into slavery."

I say it to be cruel. To punish her for her father's misdeeds. And hers.

Dahlia is the ultimate revenge fuck.

She returns her gaze to mine. I expect confusion. Tears. Refusal. Instead, she lifts her chin. "I'm not running."

And just like that, I remember why I debauched her in the first place. I enjoyed this rebellious edge–the one that separates her from the rest of them. I believed–falsely–it meant she had a soul inside that perfect shell.

I glance at the priest, who I spoke with before we walked in. He and I should understand each other perfectly now that I've lined his church pockets. "Go on."

He greets the audience. "In deference to the family's wishes, we will skip the readings and prayer and go straight to the Statement of Intentions. Antonio and Dahlia, have you come here to enter into Marriage without coercion, freely and wholeheartedly?

I nod my head. "I have."

Dahlia glances toward her parents in the front row again. Both of them vigorously nod at her. She looks over her shoulder at her bridesmaids who look as bewildered as she does. Bea, the one closest to us, shakes her head.

I cock mine and send Dahlia a warning glance. She doesn't know me–doesn't know what I'm capable of or who I am. I doubt she even knew my first name before the priest mentioned it. But she understands the look just the same. I can tell because she pales and swallows.

"I have." To her credit, her voice rings out clear and smooth.

The girl was trained to perform, and she's putting on the performance of a lifetime right now.

"Are you prepared, as you follow the path of Marriage, to love and honor each other for as long as you both shall live?"

"I am," I say.

"I am."

"Are you prepared to accept children lovingly from God and to bring them up according to the law of Christ and his Church?"

A little shock ripples through Dahlia at the mention of

children, but after another quick glance toward her parents, she answers after me, "I am."

"Since it is your intention to enter the covenant of Holy Matrimony, join your right hands, and declare your consent before God and his Church."

I reach for my virgin bride's hand and take her cold, trembling fingers. "I, Antonio Beretta, take you, Dahlia King, to be my wife."

There's a gasp in the audience at my last name.

"I promise to be faithful to you, in good times and in bad, in sickness and in health, to love you and to honor you all the days of my life."

*That's right, everyone. The Yacht King just got revenge fucked.*

Now all that remains to be done is to give his daughter the same treatment.

I expect that round will be equally if not quite a bit more enjoyable.

Dahlia says her vows like a good girl, and we exchange rings. Yes, I give her the one her intended groom bought for her. I stripped it from the young politico before I installed him and his family in a limo headed back to Manhattan under the careful guard of a few of my men. I left it to Benedict to ensure they take it gracefully once the wedding is over.

The priest pronounces us man and wife. He doesn't suggest I kiss the bride, but I take my due. I cradle the side of her flawless face and tilt her lips up toward mine.

Anger flashes in her pale eyes as I lower my head. I hover with my mouth just above hers. "Be a good girl and kiss your husband," I murmur.

"Go fuck yourself," she whispers back but lifts on her tiptoes to deliver a quick peck. She tries to draw away, but I hold her in place, slamming my lips down on hers, sliding my tongue in her mouth in front of everyone.

I hear the shocked intake of collective breaths. The murmurs grow louder as I continue to plunder my bride's mouth.

She tastes of minty toothpaste. Her lips are as soft as I remembered. Her skin as smooth. Bad on me, I guess. But kissing Jailbait didn't warrant three years in the pen.

She starts to struggle against me, pushing me away, but I hold her fast.

She needs to learn that she's not in charge of anything in this marriage. Especially not how much and well I use her pretty little body.

I ease my lips back, still cradling the side of her face in my hand. I stroke my thumb over her cheekbone. "There will be consequences for your disobedience, *Principessa.*"

She makes no sound but a little chuff of indignation bounces from her chest.

"Now smile, take my arm, and walk out of here with me. I'm the new Yacht King, and you're my prize."

I lead her straight out of the cathedral where we're showered by rice as we smile, wave, and get in the waiting limo.

"To the yacht," I command.

Benedict's wedding gift to the couple was a beautiful, new yacht named *Wedding Day* bought with my uncle's money. Now it belongs to me. I already had Benedict call to order his staff—all but the captain, who will belong to me now—off the yacht. My men are in command of the vessel. My branch of the Beretta family just got a new head-quarters.

Dahlia stares out the window in disbelief. I reach past

her to roll down the tinted glass. "Smile and wave, darling. Show them how happy you are."

I expect another *fuck you,* but other than to mutter, "I'm not your *darling,*" she does as she's told. I suppose that fits. Her rebellions are tiny–private glimpses of her will while she still outwardly performs exactly as is expected of her. As if she's incapable of stepping out of the mold created for her, no matter how much she hates it.

When we're out of sight of the throng, she turns to stare at me. "What just happened...*Antonio?*"

She spits my name out like it offends her. As if I'd kept it from her all these years.

"I just claimed my due." I sit back against the limo seat, satisfaction coursing through my veins.

Her mouth opens and closes, then opens again. "And *I'm* your due?"

"The yacht business was my due. You are the icing on the cake. The *coup de grace,* as they say."

I wonder if she marvels at my French. Wonders how that lowly waiter she let her father's men drag away the night of her ball learned any refinement. It certainly wasn't in a Parisian prep school like the one she attended. No, I got my education in prison. French was one of the many correspondence courses I took while I plotted my revenge.

I needed all the skills I could get in order to fully claim Benedict King's life.

Dahlia stares at me in utter confusion.

So. She didn't know what happened to me.

"Did you ever wonder what became of me, *Principessa?*"

Color floods her cheeks, perhaps at the memory of what I did to her in that supply closet. "Of course, I wondered!" she says hotly.

I don't believe her. Her father certainly didn't remember me or what he'd done. I honestly didn't expect Dahlia to recognize me at the altar.

"Don't pretend you thought about me." I stroke her cheek, and she pulls sharply away.

"I really don't understand what's happening. Why did you come for me? What happened to Jake? What are you holding over my parents?"

The mention of her boyfriend sets my teeth on edge. I've been throwing darts at the newspaper clippings with their photos for years now.

"In due time, *bella*."

"No. You tell me now."

"Oh, Dahlia. There is one thing I will tell you about our marriage." I issue a dangerous look. "You don't give the orders."

Anger flares in her gaze, but she snaps her mouth shut and doesn't retort. She's either too well-bred or too scared of me. For some reason, I hope it's the former.

She glances back in the direction of the cathedral. "Are we skipping the reception?"

I imagine her brain stuttering as she tries to assimilate the fact that her mother's perfectly planned wedding has been thoroughly hijacked.

"Yes, love. I'm keeping you caged until you're sufficiently under my thumb."

She reaches up and fingers her tiara, then tears it from her hair, knocking loose the locks in front. One might believe she'd spent time in the pen herself because she strikes without warning, slashing the headpiece at me like a weapon, aiming for my eyes.

I catch her wrist as the crown hits, but not before it breaks the skin on my forehead.

Her mouth forms a round "O" of shock as she stares at the blood she produced.

Grudging admiration at her pluck surfaces. I like a fighter. It makes her ultimate defeat all the sweeter.

"Ah, there's that rebellion I remembered." I keep hold of her wrist, and with my free arm, I catch her waist and pull her onto my lap. I'm momentarily unnerved by how satisfying it is to have her soft ass cradled against my cock. To feel the slender lines of her waist under the silk brocade of her dress. To catch her honey and ginger scent.

"I will punish you for that. Drop the weapon, darling."

Rather than open her fingers, she engages in a contest of strength, trying to shove the damn tiara in my face.

"Dahlia." I don't raise my voice; I lower it.

She sucks in a sharp breath, likely hearing the danger in my tone.

"Teaching you to obey will be my pleasure, but I very much doubt it will be yours."

*Dahlia*

I don't know how I got in an actual sparring match with this man.

With *Antonio*. The guy who gave me the most exciting moment of my life. The one who appears to be some kind of criminal now. Mafia, no doubt.

I should probably be petrified for my life, considering I just drew blood, but I'm not.

There's something too familiar about him, regardless of the fact that I've only been with him for a combined total of two hours. I feel safe enough, even while he's threatening me.

Perhaps it's because he pulled me on his lap first. As if he wanted me closer, not further away.

Or maybe, it's the purr in his voice when he promises retribution. Something that makes me want to know exactly what he intends to do with me if I disobey.

His bad-boy appeal is still firmly intact.

But I'm scared enough not to push.

I release my hold on the tiara.

"Good girl." He brings my bundled fingers to his lips and bites my knuckles. Not hard, but it's more than a nip. A tiny punishment. Or perhaps a warning.

I shouldn't love the sensation the words *good girl* produce in me. The warm slithering through my core. A rise in temperature. The way they make me squirm over his hard thighs. I feel the answering hardness

"You're bruising me," I complain because his fingers are still wrapped too tightly around my wrist.

He releases it, and I lift my thumb to wipe the patch of blood at his temple. He watches me with an unwavering golden gaze.

I seem to recall that gaze was exactly what made me lose all reason the last time we were together.

The time he took my hand and pulled me into a supply closet to kiss me senseless. To stroke his large hands across my bare shoulders.

But what happened between then and now, I can't fathom. I have no idea why he's here. Why he's my new husband. What happened to Jake Reese.

I try to piece it together. "You married me for my father's business?"

Antonio scoffs. "No, *Principessa.* Your father already signed that over to me. I took you because I could."

I stare at him. "But *why?*" Some dark, desperate, needy

part of me wants to hear it's because I meant something to him. The way he meant something huge and significant to me.

But that seems unlikely. What could a sheltered, spoiled fifteen-year-old girl possibly have meant to an obviously experienced young man? A guy clearly from the street with knowledge of who-knows-what kinds of sins and pleasures? That was my impression of him at the time, anyway.

He's changed, though. The bad boy has become a man, and where he seemed dangerous before, now he's deadly.

He cages my throat with his hand and uses it to turn my head this way and that, like he's examining me. Like I'm a prize horse he's thinking of buying at auction.

He runs his thumb across my lower lip. "Because *bella*. You're the reason this whole thing began. So, in a way, you're the one who made me the Yacht King."

The man speaks in riddles. I try to lunge off his lap, but he doesn't allow it.

He holds my waist fast and reaches up to pull the pins out of my hair. "You'll wear your hair down for me," he orders.

I choose to ignore the obnoxious edict and run my fingers through the front of my hair. "It's not going to look right," I tell him. Not because I believe it's my job to look the way he wants me to. More because I hate the feeling of my stiff, unnatural waves right now. I hate updos. "There's too much hairspray in it."

"Let me see." Antonio adds his fingers to the mix, combing through and arranging it to one side. He tucks a lock behind my ear.

There's a false tenderness to the gesture that makes me shiver. It's like I wish it were real. And the falseness of it frightens me.

"You'll dress for me, now."

This time, I can't hold back. "Go to hell," I snap. "I don't know what's going on, but I won't be sticking around to find out."

His expression turns to steel. "Oh you will, Dahlia. You're my wife now. And your parents' lives depend on your continued cooperation, *bella*. But please, as I suggested before, test me. Taking you in hand will be my great pleasure."

His words make me squirm. I twist over his lap. I tell myself I'm trying to get free of it, but it's possible I'm trying to alleviate the ache in my core his words produced.

"I feel sick," I complain. Just like my parents, Antonio treats me like an errant child. So I respond with petulance.

Still holding me tight with one arm, Antonio reaches for a glass bottle of sparkling water, which he opens and holds to my lips.

I try to take it from his hands, but he pulls it away, out of my reach. He doesn't bring it back to my lips until I lower my hands. I accept the drink, suddenly desperately thirsty.

The limo rolls to a stop, and Antonio waits until a man in a suit opens the back door for us. He looks like he's part of the mob, too.

Antonio hands me out and speaks to him in Italian. The man answers smoothly as Antonio alights and takes my hand.

I strain to understand their conversation, but I don't know any Italian, and my prep school Latin was too dismal to be of much use. The only language I actually acquired was French, and that's because my parents sent me to summer school in Paris.

"Come, *Principessa*." Antonio tugs me toward the yacht that was meant to be a showy wedding gift from my father to me and Jake. Something all the society pages would photograph and write about.

Seventy-five meters in length, the enormous vessel features a pool and jacuzzi tub on the exterior decks, a stunning, double-height atrium, and four interior decks. A cinema lounge and fine dining room are available for entertaining the guests who could sleep in any of the six staterooms. The master suite has vaulted beamed ceilings and largess fit for a king.

My father named her *The Honeymoon*. He showed it to me when it was finished, not because it was truly a gift to me, but so that I would memorize all the features and details. So I could extol its virtues when I gave tours of it and hosted political meetings and parties here.

I can't imagine how much he must be withering now at how things turned out. His entire fortune and his precious prize daughter–his only child–were claimed by a mafia boss. Our reputation is forever sullied by crime.

As Antonio propels me toward the yacht, I balk. Somehow I know that if I get on *The Honeymoon*, there will be no going back. It's as if the vows I swore in the church weren't real, but this will be. This is the moment when everything changes.

I cast a wild look around, hoping to see someone who works for my father or a policeman. Anyone who might help.

Antonio says nothing, but in the next moment, I'm up over his shoulder being carried down the gangway.

"Stop it!" I kick my legs. "Put me down! I'm not going with you."

Antonio ignores my protests, swinging me in the ignominious position like a sack of potatoes onto the yacht.

That's when I realize none of my father's staff is on the

ship. They've all been replaced by the mafia. Men who appear armed and dangerous.

For the first time, I'm struck by real fear. Antonio's threat to my parents' lives and their obvious terror finally register. I don't know why I wasn't properly afraid before. I think seeing the man who has starred in so many of my fantasies—a man I never expected to see again—standing at the altar muted the danger for me.

But now it registers in every cell. I feel it to the bone.

This man is dangerous. People die by his hand. And right now, my family and I are in his crosshairs.

I change my tone. "Please," I try. "I'm sorry. Antonio, please put me down."

He gives my ass a slap. "Yes, beg, darling. It's a sound I relish from your lips."

I bite back the snarky *I'm not your darling* that wants to come out and force myself to stop kicking. "Please," I try again.

Antonio carries me into the master suite and shuts the door. The interior design of the yacht was completed by none other than Caroline Ferdova, and this room was papered in silver and gold crane wallpaper with thick white shag carpet that will get dirty by the end of our first voyage.

It was decorated for my honeymoon. Red rose petals are scattered across a white bedspread.

Champagne glasses stand on the bedside table.

Antonio drops me in the center of the bed. One breast pops free of my strapless gown, and I scramble to cover it.

Oh, God.

I suddenly realize what hadn't occurred to me in the limo or at the church.

*This sham of a marriage might require consummation.*

My gaze flies to my groom's, and a shock wave of confirmation ripples through me. His lids are at half-mast, and his tongue pushes against his cheek as he devours my body in a heated gaze.

"I'm not having sex with you!" I say quickly before we get any farther.

Antonio's lips twitch. He arches one brow. "Dahlia. You are."

I scramble back on the bed, hiking the long train of my gown up to rise awkwardly to my knees. "I won't do it. You wouldn't–you won't...it would be rape!" I'm semi-hysterical now.

As if to punctuate the moment, the yacht begins to move, taking me away from any hope of rescue or salvation.

Honestly, I was far more repulsed by the idea of consummating the marriage with Jake than I am with Antonio, but I'm not giving it up like this. I won't just lie down and take it. I draw the line at–

I realize Antonio no longer appears amused. In fact, there's a dark scowl on his sexy mouth. "I won't rape you." He's gone quite still now, and I find it vastly more threatening than when he was prowling toward me. "You will give yourself to me willingly. In fact, you'll beg me to give you release."

His confidence makes goosebumps race across my skin. I hate myself for already wanting to know what exactly he might do to me that would make me beg.

"Also, you won't leave this yacht until the marriage is consummated." He walks to the bed and extends a hand. "Now come here for your punishment."

I flatten myself against the wall and let out a semi-hysterical laugh. "I don't think so."

"I'll double it if I have to come and get you."

# Chapter Three

**A**ntonio

    I have to admit, my bride is exquisite. Her dark hair falls around her shoulders, framing a pale, heart-shaped face and intelligent blue eyes. Her perfection only heightens my thrill of victory at taking her from her intended future.

I have to firm my resolve to be cruel to her. It softened the moment I touched her–that's the power of a beautiful woman.

This is how she tempted me to my demise the first time we met.

That doesn't mean I won't thoroughly enjoy taking her in hand.

I remain casual, one hand shoved in the pocket of my tuxedo pants, the other still extended to her in a gentlemanly manner.

"Last chance, Dahlia. Come and take your punishment willingly, or I'll put you on clothing restriction."

I just made that punishment up, but now that I conceived it, I desperately hope she'll rebel.

Her pale cheeks flush with a peachy-pink, but she doesn't move.

My dick punches out against the zipper of the tuxedo pants. I move swiftly, lunging across the bed to catch her, careful not to yank her or leave bruises as I haul her off.

She squirms and fights me, so I hold her in a simple restraint, my arms pinning hers to her sides, her soft backside pressed up against my lap.

After a moment, she stops struggling and twists to try to see me.

"Do I need to tie you up for your spanking, *Principessa?*"

She glares at me.

I risk releasing her, moving slowly, and she remains still. I gently turn her and push her torso over the side of the bed. "Spread your legs, *amore.*"

She doesn't obey–but I didn't expect her to. I figure it's enough she isn't trying to claw my eyes out.

I unhook the train from her gown, then draw the zipper down the back of the dress until the entire thing falls in a white poofy puddle at her feet.

She's not wearing a bra. She stands in her heels, garters, white silk stockings, and pair of white lacy panties that beg to be pulled down.

I hold my hand down between her shoulder blades and give her ass a slap–not too hard, not too soft.

Enough to make her gasp.

"When I give you an order, *Principessa,* I expect you to obey." I pop her ass again–on the other side this time.

I repeat the action, spanking her on one cheek and the other a few more times, then I hook my thumbs in the waistband of her panties and slowly draw them down to her upper thighs.

She hunches her back, keeping her face tucked into the bedcovers.

"Good girl," I praise her because she's taking it well.

And because it pleases the fuck out of me to punish her. So much more than I imagined.

When I thought about claiming Dahlia, it was solely for revenge. This society girl who was far too good for me seven years ago will now be completely under my thumb. I plan to frighten her. Cow her. Make her sorry she ever met me.

It was to punish her father, mostly, but also to teach the spoiled little rich girl a lesson.

Now that I have her in my bedroom, now that she's my wife, my desire to punish her has morphed into something... more pleasurable. Definitely dirtier.

The best revenge of all will be to complete my debauchery of this perfect socialite. Train her to obey using pain and pleasure.

I stroke her bare flesh, noting the heat I've already produced, the redness of my handprints.

She twists to look over her shoulder at me with alarm, no doubt worried I intend to claim her virginity. I answer her look with a sharp slap.

She hides her face again.

I take my time, working slowly, enjoying the spring of her flesh under my palm, the slappy sound that fills the room. I'm not causing her real pain. It's more an imposition of my will.

Dahlia gasps and wriggles, making my dick thicken, my balls grow heavy with need. But I meant what I said—I won't force her. That's a line I won't cross.

I will just have to show her everything she's been missing. Make her hot and trembly then deny her satisfaction. If

I repeat that treatment often enough, she'll come begging me for it.

I stop and slide two fingers between her legs. She's not just wet. She's *dripping*.

"Mmm. You're already slick, Dahlia. Are you enjoying your spanking?"

"What? No!" she snaps, crossing her legs.

I chuckle. "Are you trying to alleviate that ache I've produced, *bella*?"

She squeezes her inner thighs together even more tightly.

I return to spanking her, increasing the intensity until her entire ass is a lovely shade of pink.

"Open your thighs," I command.

She doesn't move.

I deliver a couple of hard swats–much harder than I was striking before–and she squeals. "Ow! Ouch! You're hurting me."

"Open, baby."

She uncrosses her legs and parts them an inch.

I slide my fingers through her juices, rewarding her with pleasure.

She holds still this time as if listening to the movement of my fingers. As if she wants more.

I take my time, slowly exploring her folds. I circle her clit. Apply more pressure. She grinds against my fingertip. I wonder if she's ever orgasmed. How closely she guarded that virginity. Did she mess around with other guys at balls? Do everything but give up her V-card?

That thought sends a spike of possessiveness through me. The desire to murder any boy who ever touched her.

I remove my fingers and give her a couple more punitive swats, even though she didn't do anything to deserve them.

"Stop it!" she cries.

"You'll take it however I give it, *Principessa*. That's the way this is going to work."

She reaches back and covers her ass. I gather her wrists at her lower back with one hand and return to my slow exploration of her folds. The tissue is already engorged, plump with excitement, blooming for me.

I listen for her quickening of breath. Find what makes her pussy clench and squeeze on air. I screw one finger into her tight entrance.

She's definitely a virgin.

She goes still, her legs shivering, her belly lifting and falling with her panting breath. I'm gentle, working my finger in and out slowly, tracing it back up to her clit, then down to enter her again in a pleasure circuit.

A small puff of breath escapes her lips. Then a moan.

But I don't give her satisfaction. I want her needy for me. Hungry.

I just give her a little taste of the pleasure I can deliver. Then I pull away. I sit beside her on the bed and tug her to sit on my lap.

"Punishment's over. You took it well." I kiss her bare shoulder, and she shivers.

"Why are you doing this?"

I stroke my palm along her bare side, relishing the feel of her soft skin. "Because I can, *Principessa*." I trace a fingertip up the inside of her thigh, and she clamps her legs tightly together. Her pussy is still slick, leaving a track of wetness on my suit pants.

Her stomach rumbles, and she puts a hand over it like she's embarrassed.

"You're hungry." I lift her off my lap, stand, and go to the door to speak to one of my men outside. When I turn back, I find Dahlia hurriedly trying to get back into her wedding dress.

"The clothing stays off." I put an edge to my voice to let her know I won't be defied.

She only tries harder to get the gown back in place to close the zipper.

"*Dahlia.*"

She freezes and meets my gaze, her lips tight, her chin at a haughty angle.

"Don't make me say it again."

Her nostrils flare, and she doesn't move for a moment, then she opens all her fingers at once and allows the weighty fabric to fall back to the floor.

"For how long?"

She's smart. Asks the right questions. She definitely has an inner brat, but she knows when to bite her tongue or bide her time. She may have been thrust into the role of insipid socialite, but I suspect she sees through the lies of her existence. She has a grasp on–or wants to see–the bigger picture.

"Until you earn them back with good behavior."

She puts her hands on her hips. I like the way she stands there, naked except for her garters, hose, and heels, and meets my gaze. I may have stripped her of her clothing, but she's not grabbing fig leaves to cover up. Her pride is still intact. Her feminine will may be flexible–she chooses her battles–but it's not weak. She's still the feisty girl who sought me out at her coming out ball.

Her eyes narrow. "I won't have sex with you."

"So you've said. But you will obey me. I know you were raised to be a good little wife. Show me you'll be that for me, and we'll get along fine."

Her eyes flash. "I was raised to be a *president's* wife," she spits. "Not a thug's."

There it is. The derision I expected from her. The belief that I'm not good enough for her. That I'll ruin her pedigree.

Well, good. That was my fucking intention.

I arch a brow. "I seem to recall you being quite hungry for a taste of *thug* the first time we met."

She flushes.

"So now you have me." I spread my arms, but there's no smile on my face. "And believe me, Dahlia, you're getting what you deserve."

She goes still, lips parting as she obviously tries to distill the meaning of my words.

As I suspected, she's not an idiot.

She stalks quickly toward me. "*How* did I deserve this? What did I do?"

I let her search me with her gaze, then I nod. "That is the mystery you must solve, no?"

*Dahlia*

I was raised to look pretty, have perfect manners, and be able to hold a conversation with anyone worthy of my attention. I also have a college degree from Smith, but it's in music appreciation. Nothing has prepared me to manage a situation like this. Just like seven years ago, it's apparent I'm completely out of my depth with Antonio.

A tap sounds on the door, and Antonio points at me. "Get under the covers, Dahlia." There's a sharpness to his tone, like me being seen naked by his staff is akin to an ambush situation.

Interesting. He wants me naked but only for his eyes.

I file that away. I need all the information I can, including all of this man's quirks and weaknesses if I'm going to get myself out of this situation.

I show my obedience, as he requested, by kicking off my heels and climbing in the bed. I pull the covers up over my breasts. My body is still aflame from his punishment. The spanking was mild–I don't think he meant to hurt me, it was more to dominate me. Humiliate me.

But my ass is tingling and warm now, and there's a hot pulsing between my legs that makes me almost sorry I declared I wouldn't have sex with my groom.

Two men come in–clearly both mafia–carrying a fully set table into the room. They remove covers from the food to reveal two plates, heaped high with a variety of foods. The delicious scent makes my stomach rumble.

A third man–also one of Antonio's–carrying a bucket with a bottle of champagne on ice.

He speaks to Antonio in Italian, and when my new husband nods, he uncorks the champagne and pours it into two tall flutes.

When the staff–or thugs, or whatever they are–have left the room, Antonio pulls out one of the chairs for me and raises his brows expectantly.

I dutifully climb out of the bed and take the offered seat. As I draw close, my breath quickens, a tingle of aware-ness racing across my skin. His eyes darken as he traces the curves of my bare breasts with his gaze. I lift my chin, refusing to allow his perusal to make me blush and quiver.

Okay, fine, I might be quivering, but I refuse to show him that.

The corners of his lips tip up.

I keep my head high as I sit in the offered seat, and he pushes it in, like a perfect gentleman.

I pretend eating with no clothes on is the norm for me. I spread my napkin over my bare lap and wait for my new husband to settle into his chair.

He picks up one of the champagne flutes. Resolved to play his game until I can learn enough to get myself out of this, I pick up mine.

"To revenge," he says.

*Revenge.* I guess I should have inferred that that was his game, but since I could think of no reason Antonio would have for revenge against me or my father, it didn't fully compute.

I hesitate, not lifting my glass to his. "Revenge for what?" I ask, even though I know he won't answer.

I watch his face as I ask the question. Rather than the glint of satisfaction, I see a stony hardness. He sets his champagne glass down without drinking from it. It's as if whatever reason he has for revenge is real. He has been harmed.

But by my father? That seems hard to believe. What would he have to do with a man like Antonio?

*Oh.*

"He did something to you." My breath gets caught up in my throat, drying it out. "My father? He did something to you at my debutante ball. What was it?"

Antonio's face remains granite. He doesn't move or speak.

Then he abruptly shucks his tuxedo jacket and removes one of his cufflinks. Slowly, methodically, he rolls up one sleeve to reveal a forearm of corded muscle. Halfway up his arm is some kind of tattoo with three cubes.

He points to it as if it means something. I have no idea what it could possibly mean.

"This is a prison tattoo."

I wait, still not understanding.

"Do you know how I ended up in prison?"

*Oh God.* I'm suddenly terribly sick. The food that had smelled so good now turns my stomach.

I blink back tears. "Not–" I choke out–"not because of me?"

Antonio gives a single nod, his whiskey-colored gaze locked onto mine.

"But...how? You did nothing wrong. Did he say you... raped me?" My voice rasps out hoarse and dry.

Antonio gives a humorless chuff. "No. That would ruin your perfect reputation, Dahlia. And then your mayor wouldn't have you. No, he concocted a story about me stealing from him and paid off three witnesses to corroborate.

"That was after his security thugs broke four ribs, my nose, my cheekbone, and three teeth."

Tears stream down my face. This can't be. No.

Yet, even though I've never seen my father show even the smallest amount of violence, I somehow know it's true. He's a ruthless businessman. He goes after his enemies and demolishes them. I just never considered that he might not stay within the lines of the law, or morality, for that matter.

"Antonio," I choke. "I had no idea, I swear. I'm so sorry."

"I believe you." He looks at me coolly. "And thank you. But honestly, your being sorry takes some of my satisfaction away. So go back to being a snobby debutante, and I'll go back to torturing you."

It takes me a moment to recover from the shock of his statement.

"For how long?"

"Hmm?"

"How long do you intend to torture me? When will it be enough to satisfy you? Is it not enough that you took King Yachts and embarrassed my father in front of all of New York society?

"Do you plan to keep me forever? I mean, how do you see this going? I'm going to have your babies? Be a good little mafia wife? Do you really want a loveless marriage?"

"Oh, that's right," Antonio says. "Are you telling me you love your precious mayor?"

My face gets hot, not with embarrassment so much as the indignity of my entire life. The fact that I never had the option of love.

"No, but I didn't have any choice! You do. Why would you willingly choose this? Don't you believe in love?"

Antonio's upper lip curls, but he says, "Sure. I believe in love. I'm doing this for love."

I'm shocked by the heat of jealousy his words produce and the bile that rises to my throat. Is there someone else? A girlfriend he had to leave behind when he went to prison? "Love for whom?" I snap.

Antonio tips his head back slightly, looking down the column of his nose at me. "My mother."

I blink. "What?"

He picks up a fork and points it toward my plate. "Eat, Dahlia."

My stomach insists I obey him, despite my emotional upheaval. I pick up my fork and dip it into a fluffy pile of mashed potatoes drizzled in a Cabernet reduction sauce. Antonio cuts into his steak and pops a piece into his mouth.

We eat silently for a few moments, and I don't think he's ever going to elaborate, but after he takes his next bite, he says, "My mother always wished for me to have a legitimate life." He takes a sip of champagne.

I pick up mine and drink down half of it.

"I was born into the Beretta family. My father died for *la Famiglia* when I was four years old. My mother wanted something different for me.

"She fought the family to keep me away from it all. That's why I was working for a catering company the night of your coming-of-age party. I could have been making bank on the wrong side of the law with my cousins, but I refused it all. I chose a legitimate path. And then I kissed the wrong girl."

My chest tightens. "I'm sorry."

"You were too big a temptation for me, I guess."

I'm annoyed by my reaction to his words—the flush of pleasure that spreads from my chest down to the junction between my two legs.

His gaze takes on a smolder. "And now you are mine. Was I the first to slip you the tongue, Dahlia?"

Now the heat spreads across my chest and up my neck. Damn this man for having such an effect on me!

"Hmm? Was I?"

"No. But—" I break off before I reveal too much. *But it was the first time I liked it. It was the first time I wanted more.*

"But what?"

I shake my head. "Nothing."

He arches a brow and waits, but there's no way I'm going to give him the satisfaction of knowing how much his kiss changed my life.

The confident way he took my jaw in one hand and plunged his tongue in my mouth. His other hand, squeezing and kneading my ass. My body pulled up tight against his muscled frame. If we hadn't been caught, I just might have given him everything that night, if he'd asked for it.

I'd considered myself a smart girl, but Antonio had turned my brain to mush with just one kiss.

"Will I be the first to put my tongue between your legs, Dahlia?"

# Chapter Four

*ntonio*

Dahlia slaps her legs together, her pupils flaring. "Don't be crass." She applies her focused intention to her steak, forcefully cutting it and stabbing it with her fork.

I can tell by her blush that I will claim that first from her as well.

Good. Despite four years at college–a *women's* college, thank fuck–she is still the sweet virgin her family purported her to be.

I sit back, enjoying her reaction to my words.

Her nipples have beaded up, and there are two spots of high color on her cheeks. She wants my head between those creamy white thighs of hers.

And now that I've mentioned it, she probably won't stop thinking about it.

"I'm not being crass, darling. I'm telling you how I will express my love in our marital bed." I take a leisurely sip of my champagne.

Dahlia downs the rest of her glass and reaches for the

bottle, which is standing in the ice bucket. She pours herself another generous glass and drinks down another four gulps.

"I can make you tremble and beg for it."

She lets out a little *puh* of air.

"I can. All I have to do is push those knees wide and part your lips with my thumbs to expose that pretty pink center for my tongue."

She blushes a deeper shade of pink, and her gaze flicks from her plate to mine three times.

"I'll swirl my tongue around your inner lips. Stroke your pleasure center. Maybe use my fingers a little. Massage your asshole as I do it."

"Stop!" Her fingers shake as she puts the next bite in her mouth. I suspect no one has spoken to Dahlia of pleasure before. Maybe she thought sex was something to be taken by a man. Something she must give up, but not enjoy. Maybe she has no idea how wonderful I can—and will—make her feel.

"Now you're just trying to get a rise out of me."

"Not trying." I smirk. "*Succeeding*. But it's all true, *amore*. I know how to please a woman. How to use my tongue in ways that will make you scream for more."

Her nostrils flare. "I don't want to hear about your exploits with other women."

There's a note of jealousy to her tone that I find deeply satisfying.

I'm certainly a jealous man. Dahlia may not have given me her heart or her body yet, but she definitely belongs to me. The sense of possessiveness I feel goes to my very core.

"No? I thought perhaps you were encouraging me to seek my pleasure outside of the marital bed. Or will you receive the pleasure I can give you?"

Her jaw thrusts forward in anger as she sets her fork down. "*No.*"

"No to which?"

"Both."

She answers immediately, sending another surge of satisfaction blasting through my chest.

"You want me to remain faithful?"

She narrows her eyes to a murderous gaze.

I want to push her into complying with my demands, but I suspect she hasn't been sufficiently tempted yet.

"You won't leave this yacht until you've spread those pretty legs for me. But I understand you're still angry. I'll give you a week, *Principessa*. A week to get used to your change in husband. After that, if you're still making me wait, I will be giving my attention to another woman."

Dahlia looks ready to throw her food in my face. "And if...if I *have* let you..."

I enjoy watching Dahlia struggle to find the words, but let her off the hook. "If I have a legitimate wife, I will be faithful to her."

I swear to Christ, I watch Dahlia's neck grow longer, her back straighter, like a flower that just found light.

"You would be a faithful husband." I hear disbelief in the statement.

I nod. "I just married a beautiful woman. Why would I stray?"

I know she likes my words because she flushes as she picks up her forks and resumes eating.

"I do intend to teach my wife all manner of pleasure," I tell her casually, like sex isn't a taboo subject at the dinner table. "I'll find what makes her squirm."

Dahlia squirms.

"What makes her scream."

Her thighs clamp together.

"I'll figure out what gets her excited and make sure she gets a dose of it every day."

She guzzles the rest of her champagne. "That's, um... that's very bold of you."

"It's not bold for a man to want to keep his wife satisfied. I will provide for you, Dahlia. Keep you in the same manner you've become accustomed to living. I'll give you what you need in bed and be faithful to you."

I say nothing of my own satisfaction for the moment. Once she's surrendered herself to me, I will make my demands. Until then, she requires a lighter touch.

"Naturally, I expect the same respect in return. You touch another man, and he dies. Remember that before you curse a man to his death."

\* \* \*

*Dahlia*

Antonio gives me a chilling smile, and a shiver runs up my spine at his threat.

I believe him. I believe this man is a killer. I shudder to think of the crimes he's committed. The darkness that surrounds him.

And he wants my name to be attached to his for the rest of our lives.

*No, thank you.*

No way.

I have to find a way out of this.

I toss my napkin over the plate and stand. My dramatic exit is diminished greatly by the fact that I'm naked and, therefore, have nowhere to go.

But my suitcase should've been brought to the yacht

yesterday in preparation for our honeymoon. I pull open one of the drawers and find my clothing neatly folded and put away. I pull out a pair of panties.

Antonio tsks. "We're working on obedience, *Principessa*. I didn't say you could wear panties."

I'm too cowed by him at the moment to put up a fight, so instead, I throw the panties on the floor like a spoiled child and stalk into the bathroom.

I could use a shower, anyway.

I need to wash this day off of me. Get my bearings. Figure out my next move.

I shut the door and lock it and take the world's longest shower. When I'm finished, I take another half an hour to brush out my hair, apply lotion, and generally stall.

I half-expect Antonio to demand I come out or demand admittance, but he leaves me alone.

Finally, when I've grown sick of the small quarters, I emerge with a towel wrapped firmly up to my armpits.

The dinner table and champagne bucket have been removed.

Antonio lounges on the bed with his ankles crossed reading a newspaper. He's still in his tuxedo pants, but the tie is gone, and his crisp white shirt is unbuttoned at the collar. I hate how devastatingly handsome he looks.

This man is a thug who spent time in prison, yet he looks every inch the aristocrat. I hate to admit it, but he embodies "Yacht King" so much more than my father did. I imagine he will run a ruthless business. Probably get us back into the black.

*Us.* I don't know why I'm saying *us*.

It's not my family's business anymore, and I'm not sticking with Antonio to make it mine through him.

"Are you sleeping in here?" I ask doubtfully. I mean, I

guess that's obvious. He's my husband. We share a bed. He wants to consummate.

It's just that I hadn't considered how it would feel to climb under the covers–*naked*–with this extremely good-looking, muscular, and well, *virile* man.

Not that I'm tempted to consummate.

I'm not.

It's just...awkward to say the least.

Antonio uncrosses his ankles and sets the newspaper down on the bedside table. He stands from the bed and throws the covers back. "Are you ready for bed, darling?"

"Don't call me that," I snap, not moving any closer to the bed.

"What, *darling*? Why not?"

"Because you don't mean it."

"No, I suppose I don't," he admits. "I am taunting you." His gaze holds a challenge.

I meet it. I don't know what it is about this man that makes me bold.

I was bold that night of my debutante ball when I demanded a drag from his cigarette.

I was bold when I took his hand and let him pull me into the supply closet for the most sinful kiss of my life.

Now, another surge of rebellion rises in me, and I drop my towel. "And I'm taunting you."

The move has its desired effect.

Antonio's gaze jerks to my breasts, then travels lower, to the downy patch of hair between my legs. His jaw clenches and nostrils flare. "That's a dangerous game, Dahlia." His voice is soft. Soft enough to make me shiver with the implied threat.

It occurs to me that I've bitten off far more than I can chew. Still, I hold my ground, shoulders squared, breasts presented for his admiration. "You said you wouldn't rape me."

He prowls around the bed to my side.

It takes all my courage to hold my ground. To not bolt for the bathroom and lock the door once more.

He stalks closer and with each step, my heart picks up speed. My hands are clammy by my sides. My mouth is suddenly flooded with saliva, as if Antonio is something delectable to eat.

"It looks to me," he rumbles in a deep purr, "that you're begging to be touched."

He arrives in front of me and brushes the backs of his knuckles over the tip of my beaded nipple.

I can't suppress the shock of pleasure that ripples through me. The outward shiver that gives me away.

"Do you want me to touch you, Dahlia?" He pinches my nipple lightly between two of his knuckles and tugs. "Do you want me to show you the kind of pleasure I was describing over dinner?"

My breath comes in with tiny gasps and pants.

"N-no." I'm not very convincing. The truth is, now that he's standing here before me, over six feet of glorious muscle and man, I *do* want him to touch me.

I want to find out *exactly* what he meant about pleasuring me with his tongue.

I'm not completely ignorant nor innocent. I certainly know how to use my own fingers to bring myself pleasure. I've used a pillow between my legs at night.

And every single time I was fantasizing about this man right here.

And now to find out that he does hold all the sexual secrets I imagined, that I may not have built him up to be something he wasn't, it's all just too much.

One of Antonio's large hands settles on my hip, and the warmth of his roughened palm against my skin generates heat in my core. He continues to tease my nipple. It's starting to burn and tingle, making me needy for more.

Between my legs, there's an answering pulse. Hot, tender neediness that squeezing my thighs together doesn't alleviate. He trails his fingers lightly over my hip, then down the side of my thigh.

I try to suppress the trembling that started in my legs.

His fingertips trace up my buttocks. "Do you think your precious mayor could make you feel this way, Dahlia?"

"He's not my precious mayor," I choke out. I don't know why I give Antonio the satisfaction, though.

Antonio shifts his fingers from my nipple to lightly trace up the column of my neck until his index finger arrives at my chin. He gently nudges it up until I look him in the eye. "No?"

I find myself shaking my head. "It was an arranged marriage."

"Like ours," he says as if satisfied.

"This was not an arranged marriage. You stole me from my groom!"

As soon as I speak the words, I wish I hadn't because Antonio's face darkens, and he takes a step back from me. I immediately register the loss of his touch. Crave his attention.

"Ah, yes. A groom far more worthy of the yacht princess. Too bad. You're cursed to slumming with a blue collar brute for the rest of your days, *Principessa*."

My stomach knots as I realize the bitterness in Antonio's tone is borne of the degradation and treatment he received at the hands of my father and our penal system.

I'm sure the jury took one look at the working-class son

of Italian immigrants and assumed he'd done everything my father accused him of.

"I don't believe you're a thief, Antonio." I make my voice soft. Conciliatory.

Antonio's eyes narrow. He holds my jaw with an over-hand grip "You should." He brings his face close to mine. So close I feel the heat of his breath feathering over my lips. "Believe it, Dahlia. Know that I'm going to keep on stealing from you for the rest of your life."

# Chapter Five

*ntonio*

"*Buongiorno*," Angelo, one of my hired servants murmurs, rushing to my side when I crack an eye against the sun.

Fuck. Did I pass out on the deck last night?

I'm sprawled in a chaise lounge, my white tuxedo shirt unbuttoned to my chest.

Angelo holds a tray with various juice options–orange, grapefruit, tomato. Or is that a Bloody Mary? My stomach turns. I reach for the orange juice.

"Ham and cheese omelet with sourdough toast," I order. I don't even know what food is on this boat, but I assume they can figure that out.

"*Si signore.*"

"Make one for my bride, as well."

"She has already eaten, sir."

For some reason, that answer irritates the piss out of me. Whether it's because my bride ate without me or because I have a bride now, I'm not sure.

If I weren't still a vengeful fuck, I would get rid of

Dahlia quickly. Deposit her in my place in the Hamptons and take up residence in the loft on Billionaire Row. I could visit her a few times a month to get her pregnant. Once she's pregnant, she could be shut away for good. I would only require her to trot out and accompany me to society events once every few months.

I wouldn't have this need to continue stealing from her. To take and take until there's nothing of her left that doesn't belong to me–her body, her mind, her will.

I did allow her to sleep alone last night. After she reminded me how beneath her I am–that I stole her from her legitimate fiance, I left her in our master suite and spent the night drinking myself into a stupor. That's how I ended up waking on the deck of my newly acquired yacht.

The sound of a helicopter flying overhead gets me onto my feet and reaching for a gun.

My men emerge from all directions, holding machine guns all pointed toward the approaching helicopter.

"Put the weapons away." My bride strides onto the deck in a short mini-dress and wide-brimmed sun hat with a large navy bow at the back and a pair of huge sunglasses.

Before the thought has even reached my brain, I'm running for her, needing to get her safely below deck.

I pull up short when my tiny wife lifts an arm gaily in the air and waves at the helicopter with a broad, Hollywood smile on her face. "Smile and wave, Antonio," she says between bared teeth. "That's the press."

The...*what?*

I twist to look up at the helicopter. My brain and body are still telling me this is an attack, but I realize she must be right. If they were going to shoot at us, they would've done it by now.

I did just hijack the wedding of New York's most

famous belle. It makes sense that the press might be here to try to catch us on our honeymoon and figure out how this all happened.

"Guns away," I snap, tucking my own back in the holster at my ankle.

I put my arm around my prize wife and join her in a jaunty wave.

It occurs to me that she could've sent up a distress signal. Waved both arms or somehow looked frantic and in need of rescue. The fact that she directed my men to hide their weapons and look appropriate surprises me.

I'm not dumb enough to believe she's on board with this wedding or even that she intends to be compliant. At least she's doing her duty at the moment.

The helicopter circles the yacht, and I verify that she's right—a camera lens winks in the sun.

"Give them a good show, princess." I wrap my other arm around her and bend her backward in a dip, then kiss the fuck out of those lush lips of hers.

She goes still, shocking me by accepting the kiss. I sense the thump of her heart against my chest as she begins to move her lips against mine. I thrust my tongue in her mouth, sweeping it boldly, fucking her with it. My dick thickens and stretches along my leg, pressing into her belly.

And then I don't want to stop. I no longer give a shit about the helicopters or the reporters. I don't care what kind of photos they get.

All I want is to conquer the beautiful debutante who thinks she's too good for me. She may believe I'm beneath her, but that doesn't change the fact that her body responds to me. That her curiosity over what I could give her, what I could make her feel, never died.

I'm suddenly locked in and laser-focused on only one

goal: winding up my new wife. Making sure she's hot and needy and desperate for what I can give her.

And I can't fucking wait until I know exactly what that pretty face of hers looks like when she comes.

I slide one of my hands down to her ass, kneading the soft flesh there. This is how I lost myself last time.

When the delicate blue-blood proved that she may look like she's made of porcelain, but hot blood runs in her veins.

My kiss loses finesse and turns aggressive with passion.

It's the way she responds to me–that gasp of excitement, the offering of her lush body to my hands. She heats beneath my touch. I lift her upright, so I can get at her neck, kissing and nibbling down the slender column.

"Oh." Her little gasp of surprise gets me harder than granite. I slip my forearm under her ass and boost her ass up so I can carry her to the closest wall. Her legs part to straddle my waist, sending the short minidress careening up her thighs.

If I weren't half out of my mind, I would worry how much of her delicious thighs my men can see. Or the photographers for that matter.

But I've forgotten there's anyone else around. I've forgotten my revenge. I've forgotten everything but the taste of her mouth and the feel of her lush body. The excited sounds that leave her throat.

I pin against the wall and deepen the kiss. It's all teeth and tongue and bruising force. My erection presses against her belly. I drop her ass lower into my hands to line the notch between her legs up with my throbbing member.

She moans against my mouth. I thrust my tongue in rhythm with the rock of my hips, a slow fuck.

"*Antonio,*" she gasps.

Fuck.

I must be losing my mind because I would give up this yacht just to hear her say my name in that desperate, breathy tone again. To hear her chant it over and over like an invocation. Like she's praising God.

"That's right, *Principessa*." I bite down on her neck. "This is how your husband is going to take care of you." I lick the place I bit, then suck. "Every. Fucking. Day."

"Antonio." She's panting. Rocking her hips to meet my thrusts. I find the waistband of her panties and yank them down her ass, dying to get that small scrap of fabric out of my way, so I can give it to her hard. Right here, right now.

Dahlia panics.

Suddenly, she's kicking and shoving me away, wriggling and scrambling to get out of my arms.

I return to my senses.

Easing Dahlia back to her feet, I pull up her panties and adjust the hem of her dress. I give her ass a pat. "No, dear. Not until you beg me for it."

She huffs, rolling her eyes and giving my chest a shove.

Hearing the beat of the helicopter's blades, I pull her against my body as if she were trying to hug me instead. She allows it, and I hold her for a few counts before I release her.

"You will beg, darling." I adjust her sunhat, which I must've knocked askance when I was kissing her. Her lips are swollen and puffy from the kiss, her cheeks flushed.

It makes me hungry for Round Two.

"Don't hold your breath, Antonio." she shoots back, flouncing away. Then she stops and twists to look at me over her shoulder. "On second thought, do. I could definitely survive the tragedy of a marriage cut short by an early death."

\* \* \*

*Dahlia*

As I walk away from Antonio, my body buzzes from his kiss. My panties are soaked, nipples hard beads beneath my bra cups.

I don't know how he does it to me. Why I find him so achingly attractive. I can't fathom what it is about him that makes me desperate for his attention.

Maybe the real appeal of the bad boy is that he doesn't give a crap about me. It calls to that human desire to win friends and make connections. He's the ultimate challenge.

It makes sense. I met him at a ball where everyone had to be polite to me, if not fawning.

And there he was. Watching me with total disinterest. Derision, even.

And I just had to make him want me.

Sadly, I'm still that fifteen-year-old girl.

Antonio claimed me to punish my father. He thinks I'm a spoiled rich girl. He has no real interest in me, and yet I'm dying to make him fall in love.

To win over the bad boy and prove I am worthy.

It's that realization, more than anything, that strengthens my resolve to get myself out of this unhealthy, dangerous situation.

There has to be a way to unbind myself from Antonio.

I realize I'm walking swiftly across the length of the yacht with no particular destination in mind, other than getting away from Antonio. I end up near the helm and through the window of the console, I'm startled to see a face I recognize.

Shawn Hennessey, my father's yacht captain.

It's funny how in dire circumstances a familiar face—one

that normally would only cause me to feel a shrug of boredom—could fill me with such pleasure.

"Shawn!" I beam the first smile that's cracked my face in at least thirty-six hours.

"Dahlia!" He flicks a nervous glance in both directions, then cracks open the door to the cockpit and pulls me through it and into a hug. Then he whisper-hisses in my ear, "Your father sent me a message for you. He said he's going to get us both out of this."

Hearing footsteps outside, I pull myself out of his grasp. "It's good to see you!" I say loudly.

Antonio growls behind me, "Hands off *my wife,* or I will cut them off and throw them to the fucking sharks."

*His wife.*

The words send shockwaves through my body.

"Antonio!" I jerk back, putting at least three feet between me and the captain. "Stop. He's a family friend—I mean, an employee, that's all."

I thank God for Antonio's apparent jealousy. It seems to have distracted him from realizing Shawn passed me a message.

"He's nothing to you." Antonio says it like a warning. "You come near this *stronzo* again, and I will throw him overboard. Are we clear?"

It's perfect. I should be terrified. Appalled. But something warm slithers through my chest.

Antonio's alpha male possessiveness is over the top and absurd. But in addition to it serving as a distraction, it gets me hot. I like him staking his claim over me. It turns me on. I craved this man's attention, and now I have it. And with it comes a sense of power.

I place my hand in the center of his chest and give him a push. He allows me to back him out of the cockpit.

"Relax. I was just saying hello."

Antonio's face is still twisted in a scowl.

"You basically abducted me. You took me from my family onto a vessel with complete strangers. It shouldn't shock you that I'd be happy to see a familiar face."

Some of his irritation seems to ease.

He pulls me toward him and tucks me under his arm to escort me toward our bedroom. "Don't speak to him again."

I refuse to agree.

"Dahlia," he warns. "Do you want him dead?"

This is too much. I stop, digging my heels in, so Antonio has to stop, too. "You can't kill everyone I talk to."

He raises his brows and pierces me with a cold gaze. "Try me. You're my wife. I would murder anyone who touches or disrespects you."

I shiver. "You really are a monster, aren't you?"

His expression contorts, the cold mask breaking to show that I hit a nerve, but then he quickly recovers. "I am what your family made me."

I scoff. "My family isn't mafia. *Yours* is." I lift my nose in the air and take on a goody-two-shoes air. "Blaming others for your own failings is a bad look on you."

"And stuck-up snob is a bad look on you."

I hide my wince. I knew that's what he thought of me, but it still wounds me to hear him say it out loud.

"So, exactly who am I allowed to speak to on this yacht?" I demand.

Antonio hesitates. "No one. No one but me."

I throw my hands in the air and start marching toward the sun deck. "That's absurd. You are absolutely insane."

"Don't test me," he warns, but I've already made up my mind.

I'm definitely about to call his bluff.

I stride up to a grouping of his men standing near the rails. He's not going to throw his mafia soldiers overboard when I speak to them.

"Hi guys." I try out my flirty voice. "I don't think we've been properly introduced." I touch the nearest guy on the shoulder and step close. "I'm Dahlia."

"Get away from her," Antonio barks.

In the next moment, I find myself flung over his shoulder. My short dress rides up to my waist, no doubt giving the men a view of my panty-clad ass. "Don't look at her," Antonio roars as he stomps away. My trunk swings behind his back.

Instead of taking me to our bedroom, he walks into one of the other staterooms–apparently an uninhabited one– and deposits me on the crisply-made queen-sized bed.

He towers over me, but rather than finding his large, imposing visage intimidating, I'm turned on by the caveman display of possessiveness. My gaze tracks his large hands curled into fists at his sides, how good he looks, even in yesterday's rumpled tuxedo.

"Clothing restriction." Antonio's voice is a choked growl, his dark brows slash down. He tugs my dress up over my head. He doesn't hurt me, but his movements are rough and jerky.

Gone is the smooth, revenge-is-a-dish-served-cold man who ordered me about in cool, manicured tones last night.

This man feels more raw. More real.

I'm totally turned on. I'm also far more wary of him. I don't want to anger the bull. I allow him to strip me of my bra and panties. I even kick off my sandals myself–a show of surrender.

Antonio stoops to pick up my dress, panties and bra. He points a finger at me. "I warned you."

I scramble up off the bed, so I'm not in such a submissive position. I try to think of something clever to say in return, but nothing comes to mind.

As it turns out, I'm saved from answering because Antonio marches out of the room.

I stand there, naked, contemplating the situation.

Then I realize the solution is simple. Antonio doesn't like me talking to other men, he doesn't want them looking at my ass, and he took away my clothing.

He literally walked right into this one.

I stride to the door and pull it open. Then I strut out like I own the place.

\* \* \*

*Antonio*

Oh, *hell no.*

I lurch forward at a dash when I catch sight of my fully naked bride and her fuck-hot body arriving on deck in full view of all of my men.

I was an idiot. I should have known she has more spunk than shame about her nudity.

I'm not sure my feet even touch the ground as I cross the deck to catch her. Wrapping an arm around her waist, I pull her into the air, spin her around, and head for the master suite.

"You love punishment, don't you, *Principessa*?" I murmur growl against the shell of her ear.

"Controlling you just became my number one pastime."

*Controlling* me? I grit my teeth. "We'll see who controls who." She wants to use her body to control me? I will use it against her.

I know she's curious about sex. I will have her begging in no time.

I will punish the fuck out of her with orgasms until she weeps for me to give her my cock.

"Who controls *whom*," she corrects.

Right. Putting me in my place again. "Sorry, my prison education didn't quite compare to your prep school," I growl.

I carry her straight to the closet where I pull out a belt.

That scares her. She goes wild in my arms, thrashing and kicking. I manage to keep hold of her until I get her to the bed where I pin her wrists above her head and lash the belt around them.

She quiets somewhat, no doubt relieved I'm not going to whip her with it.

I lash the end of the belt to the bedpost. Then I stand on my knees to observe.

My bride looks beautiful, her dark hair spread in a fan around her flushed face. Her perfect tits are lifted and spread, her nipples a dusky-rose against her pale skin.

I run my thumb across my lower lip admiring her. "I like you bound," I observe. "I might just keep you this way for the rest of the trip."

She thrashes her legs, twisting her hips this way and that. "Let me go!"

"Oh, no, sweetheart. We have your punishment to deal with first."

Her lips close, and she stares at me.

"Not going to ask what it is?"

"I'm sure you're about to tell me."

I shrug. "Nah. I'll just let you experience it." I grip her thighs and push her knees wide, all the way up to her shoulders.

Her belly flutters. "Wh-what are you doing?"

"Looking at what's mine."

It's a beautiful pussy. Pristine. Unpenetrated by another man. My usual type of woman is one with more experience, but I relish the idea of being Dahlia's first.

Make that her *only*.

Because she is mine now. And mine alone.

Which means her beautiful body belongs to me.

Her orgasms belong to me.

Her freedom belongs to me.

I may not be able to take her heart, but I will rule the rest of her like the fucking boss that I am.

She tries to close her knees, to push them out of my hands, but I hold her fast, just drinking in the sight of her. Letting her feel my dominance. My ownership. My desire.

Taking my time, I lower my head and drag the tip of my tongue along her slit.

Her anus contracts, and she jerks against my hold.

I explore her soft folds with no particular goal other than tasting her. Getting acquainted with her terrain. Her reactions to my touch.

Her breath draws in soft pants, her inner thighs start to quiver. Within seconds, her juices are flowing, and I lap them up with my tongue.

"You said you wouldn't have sex with me."

"This isn't sex. This is punishment," I tell her, even though it's quite obviously something far more pleasurable than my other forms of chastisement. The punishment will come when I leave her hanging. When I get her wet and ready, blooming for my entrance, and then I back off.

She mewls softly when I trace along her inner lips, then swirl up to her clit and suck.

I continue my slow torture, penetrating her with my

tongue, sucking her labia, nipping. My cock is heavy, aching to be inside her.

Dahlia tugs against the belt, squirming against my mouth. No, pressing up into it.

She's definitely enjoying herself now.

I keep at it, building her right to the edge, judging by the pitch of her moans, and then I draw back.

For a moment, she doesn't move. Then her head snaps up. "What's happening?" she sounds alarmed.

"What do you want to happen, Dahlia?"

Her head falls back, and her eyelids flutter closed. "Oh, God."

I wait.

Her eyes pop back open, glassy and large. Frantic. "Are you going to finish?"

"How would you like me to finish, princess?"

"Wh–what you were doing was fine. I mean, if that's my punishment."

I chuckle and shake my head. "No, this is your punishment." I back all the way off the bed.

She draws in an angry gasp when she realizes. "No. You can't leave me here like this. You *can't*."

I give her a cool smile. "I can, dear wife. This is what happens when you challenge me."

I step into the bathroom and strip out of the stale tuxedo to take a much-needed shower.

When I walk out, Dahlia's body's gone limp. Her knees hang open like butterfly wings, and her head is turned to the side.

"Please–my wrists are hurti–" The last syllable dies on her lips when she takes in my bare torso, still glistening with water droplets from the shower. Her gaze traces my pectoral muscles down my abs to the white towel around my waist.

I'm tempted to taunt her with my body, but then, I remember her innocence, so I ignore her and stride to the dresser where my clothing has been unpacked with hers. With my back turned to her, I drop the towel and pull on a pair of boxer shorts, feeling the heat of her gaze on me the entire time.

I turn and let her eye the erection tenting the soft cotton. I probably should have beat off in the shower to take the pressure off, but my pride wouldn't let me. I want to come inside my bride. I'm saving every last drop for her juicy cunt, so I can fill that belly with our child.

She draws in a breath and licks her lips.

"How's that pussy of yours?" I advance on the bed.

She snaps her knees closed with a soft slap of flesh.

I tsk. "Bad girl. You don't hide it from me. I own that pussy now." I grasp behind her knees and lift her feet off the bed to spread her legs wide. This time I let them come back to the bed outside my shoulders. I slide my hands under her ass and lift it slightly to meet my face.

"No-o, Antonio," she moans. "Please."

I lick into her. "Please what, darling?"

"I...I...Please don't do this."

I drag my tongue up and down her slit. I'm sloppier this time because it's hard to focus with blue balls.

No matter, she's already desperate. The moment my mouth connects with her, she tightens her ass and pushes into me, greedy for her release.

"You have no say in this," I tell her. "You chose to show your body—*the body I now own*—to my men. This is the punishment I've chosen for you."

"I...don't even understand it," she complains.

I chuckle against her soft flesh then nip her labia. "Your body does, though, doesn't it?"

"My body..." she pants. "My body wants..."

"I know what your body wants, *amore*. I can give you what you desire."

"No," she says. "No, no, no, no." Her needy tone doesn't match the words, but, of course, I honor her words.

Eventually, she will cave to me.

Instead, I continue with my slow, deliberate torture, bringing her to the brink of orgasm and back away again.

She lets out a dry sob when I climb off the bed. "You're a horrible person."

"I can be quite cruel," I agree. "You'd be wise to stay on my good side." I give her a cool smile. "And believe me, darling. This was my good side."

* * *

*Dahlia*

Antonio tortures me for hours with his tongue, driving me nearly insane. Never letting me actually reach a climax.

Finally, when I beg him for mercy, he releases my wrists from the belt.

I should be thrilled to have the use of my arms and hands back, but I get pins and needles from the blood rushing back to them and worse–much worse–is the fact that Antonio is getting dressed.

Like he's finished with me.

Like he's not going to give me the satisfaction I need.

I waste no time. As soon as I have feeling back in my hands, I roll to my belly with my hand tucked between my legs. My hips buck against the firm contact–the pressure I'd been desperate for.

The relief is so great that I moan out loud as my internal muscles clench and lift. A giant star blooms and bursts behind my eyes. I undulate my fingers and bring on a second smaller contraction, but before I'm finished, Antonio rolls me to my back.

He stares down at me, his golden eyes dark and glittering. "Did I say you could come?"

My brain doesn't even process what he's saying. I'm dizzy from my release. Lost in outer space. I blink up at him, still moving my fingers to eke out more aftershocks.

He catches my wrist and replaces my fingers with his. "This pussy belongs to me, remember?"

He moves his fingers expertly, finding the exact place I need to bring on another full orgasm.

I cry out with the release, arching up from the bed, completely at his mercy. When I blink open my eyes, I find Antonio watching me intently as he continues to slowly move his fingers.

"I didn't give you permission to come."

"Ahhhh." I'm mindless. Brainless. I have zero control over my body. Certainly no ability to refuse when he screws one thick finger inside me.

I groan because it feels so good. So right. I've used my own fingers between my legs in the privacy of my bedroom since I was a child, but this–this sensation, like his tongue–is completely beyond any pleasure I was able to give myself.

I'm shocked by how wet I am, my arousal soaking his finger, making a slick sound as he pushes it in and out. He gets deeper, bumping my inner wall, and I shriek at the sensation–a sudden loss of control–a catapulting over the edge into still more pleasure. I gush more liquid. He doesn't relent, he keeps pumping his finger, then adds a second one, making me scream and shake in the throes of incredible release. Tears stream down my face.

"Please," I beg because I can't take any more. He's been

torturing me for hours now, and the sensations are too much. I'm a rag doll. Boneless. Barely capable of putting together the thought to speak. "Please, Antonio. Have mercy."

Abruptly, he stops, slipping his fingers out and bringing them to his mouth to suck.

"I control your orgasms now, Dahlia. You don't come without me giving them. Understand?"

"Yes," I nod. I would agree to anything he said at this moment.

He wanted to prove he controls me and my body, and he has.

I pant, unable to move, my hands limply resting on my ribs. He studies me a moment longer, then nods. "Good girl."

My belly flutters. I don't care about his praise. I mean, I shouldn't. But somehow, it still has an effect on me.

"You may dress and move around the yacht as you please."

I should hate his presumed authority over me, but instead the words wash over me. I imagine I detect warmth in his tone, but it's probably just the reverberation of bliss from my orgasm.

"Go to hell," I manage to mutter as he steps out of the room.

He pauses and looks back in, and my pussy clenches as if anticipating further torture. But instead, amusement flickers on his expression. "Keep fighting me, little wife. I enjoy taking you in hand."

# Chapter Six

*ntonio*

*Fuck. Me.*

My wife emerges from our bedroom in a sexy, slinky red cocktail dress. It hugs her curves, with an open triangle cutout at her breasts and a short hemline that shows off her long, shapely legs. Her hair is curled, and she's wearing fake eyelashes and red lipstick. There's a softness about her face, like she's still riding the high from the orgasms this afternoon.

I'll say one thing—what she lacks in charm, she makes up for in looks. Our children will be beautiful.

I shouldn't think of baby-making, though, because my already blue balls grow heavy.

I stand from the table where I was going over the books. "You look beautiful."

There's a flicker of surprise on her face. I remember the same flicker at her debutante ball. As if she finds the compliment unexpected. Although surely she must be complimented every day of her life.

Perhaps it's that she doesn't expect it from me–the cretin.

I extend my hand. "Ready for dinner, *Principessa?*"

Hours ago, I had food sent to the room and left outside the door with a knock. There's no way I would risk my server entering the bedroom without me there to ensure he didn't look at her. I was told she barely touched the food, though.

"Yes. I'm starving."

For some reason, it pleases me that I get to be the one to feed her. Like it satisfies some biological caveman need to provide.

I escort her to the dining room where the table is already set for us, and my men bustle around to light candles and pour wine.

I lift my glass after hers has been poured. "To my wife. Who tastes as exquisite as she looks."

Dahlia rolls her eyes and drinks without clinking my glass.

"I enjoyed watching you come undone this afternoon."

A visible shiver runs through her. "This isn't polite dinner conversation."

I give her a stiff smile. "And yet here you are, the yacht princess, married to a man who doesn't give a fuck what you think is polite."

She recoils slightly, and I regret my sharpness. I was enjoying seeing her soft and relaxed. I don't need to poke her this way. Not after she surrendered to me this afternoon.

Of course, I hadn't given her much of a choice.

But the truth is, if she'd been frightened, or angry, or resistant, if her pussy had been dry or her body tense, I wouldn't have gone on.

No, my feisty bride enjoyed my touch and my tongue. She was incredibly responsive, and watching her come was the most spectacular sight I've seen. It was beautiful.

"Talking about your pussy at dinner is as much my right as tasting it," I declare. "And," –I pause to take a sip of my wine– "I can't wait to taste you again."

She lifts her lashes to meet my gaze. "As punishment." She doesn't say it as a question, but she's watching me like she's trying to discern how and when it will happen again.

I shrug. "It can be a reward, too. Depends on the context, I suppose."

I watch a pretty flush color the exposed triangle of skin above her breasts.

"Would you like me to describe what a reward might be like?"

She licks her lips, and the sight of her tongue gets me harder than steel.

"Hmm?" I prompt when she doesn't reply.

She takes two healthy sips of her wine. "Sure." I love how she tries to make it sound casual, but the word wobbles on the end.

"When you're good, my sweet wife, I will reward you. I'll take you to our bedroom and light a few candles. Pour you a glass of champagne. Then I'll undress you slowly, my fingertips trailing across your soft skin."

Goosebumps rise on her arms. One of my men serves two plates loaded with T-bone steak, twice-baked potatoes, and asparagus. I pause until he's gone.

"I'll pick you up and lie you on the bed. Maybe trail a rose across your bare skin to prime you for my touch."

Dahlia had been applying herself to cutting her steak, but she goes still now, raising her gaze to mine. Then she seems to shake herself out of reverie and conjures a sniff. "A rose?"

"If I can't find a dahlia," I amend with a smirk.

I see the twitch of a smile on her lips before she hides it with a bite of steak.

"And then, I'll push your knees wide and bury my head between your thighs. You'll have use of your hands this time, so you can use them to pull my hair or tug me forward."

Dahlia swallows her steak with an audible gulp.

"Of course, I'll let you come. I won't make you wait. I'll bring you to orgasm as many times as you like."

Dahlia's back straightens as if she's just squeezed her thighs together under the table. "So, Antonio, I get that you wanted revenge on me and my father, but isn't it far more of a hassle to keep me?"

I don't allow her to change the topic. "Shall I tell you what will happen if I have to punish you again?"

"No." The syllable is mulish.

"Next time I will focus my attention on your ass."

Dahlia stops chewing.

"The next time I spank you will be over my knee. A more intimate experience for both of us."

"Stop talking," Dahlia snaps, the color high on her cheeks.

"I will turn your ass pink before I give that tight little rosebud between your cheeks my full attention."

"*Antonio.*" Shock laces the syllables.

I give her a wicked smile. "Don't worry, darling. It can be just as satisfying as having me between your legs. Over time, you will come to beg me to fuck you there, as well."

Dahlia's fork hand shakes on the way to her mouth. "Let me go, Antonio. Please."

I shake my head. *"Never."*

She gets up from the dinner table, throwing her napkin down over her plate.

I stand when she does, like a gentleman. I studied and practiced refined etiquette from the moment I got out of prison. Not because Benedict King called me a brute. Not to prove him wrong. Because he was right–I am a brute. A complete monster.

No, it was a necessary adoption to enact my revenge plan. To get myself in the right doors. It's been a very long con to lure Benedict King into investments then arranging the default of those investments. Ultimately offering him the loan on the behalf of Don Beretta.

She leaves the table, and I let her go.

My satisfaction at goading her doesn't taste as juicy as I'd hoped. Nor does eating the rest of my dinner alone.

\* \* \*

*Dahlia*

Ugh. That man. I'm trembling when I get back to the room, angry and hot and just as needy as I was this afternoon before Antonio got me off.

I seriously want to kill that man. I should have taken one of those steak knives at the table and dug out his heart with it.

Except then he wouldn't be alive to use that glorious tongue between my legs. He wouldn't be able to smirk at me and make me feel beautiful and coveted and dirty all at the same time.

I can't deny the effect he has on me. It's no less potent than it was at my debutante ball seven years ago. Just being in his presence electrifies me.

I strip out of the dress I wore to taunt him and put on a sleep shirt. I dig out the mystery novel I packed back when I thought I would be on my honeymoon with a man who bored me.

Books have always been my distraction, my best friend when I felt alone. But at this moment, even reading doesn't work for me. I can't get lost in the story or the characters' lives. All I can think about is those smoldering golden eyes staring at me across the dinner table. The way Antonio held his wine glass in that large hand of his swirling the contents as he studied me. As he tempted me.

I do admit that I love his temptation. I love that he's intent on seducing me—his wife. He could just as easily have forced me to marry him and locked me in a cabin on the yacht somewhere. Or worse, he could have forced himself on me. He seems the type of man who's forced a great number of people to do his bidding.

The fact that he remains a gentleman with me and is waiting for me to give him permission to take my virginity, both titillates and soothes me.

Yes, I'm still enamored with the silly notion of reforming the bad boy. Of softening the heart of a hardened man. It's the fantasy that got me in trouble at my debutante ball.

When my father opened that closet door and found me with Antonio's lips locked on mine, one large hand cupping my ass and one squeezing my breast, he shamed me so thoroughly, I never really recovered. My parents took away all the birthday gifts I received from the ball, and I wasn't allowed to go to Paris for the next two summers.

It became the event my parents threw at me every time I stepped out of line. My mom would get tight-lipped and warn me against ruining the family as I'd nearly done then. My father would threaten to disown me if I ever did.

And I guess, in a way, I have.

No, *screw that!*

This was all my father's doing. What he did to Antonio was unconscionable. He had no right to treat him like dirt. Not that it excuses Antonio's grandiose revenge plot.

I should be more disturbed than I am about what it says about the kind of man he is. That he could harbor such a grudge to have enacted such an elaborate plan. I have to admire it, though. It took a brilliant man to bring down my father. To climb as high as Antonio obviously has and capture an entire yacht business and the daughter of the socialite in one swoop.

After a couple of hours, I give up on the book. I decide to try out the oval marble bathtub in the bathroom. Filling it with hot soapy water, I strip out of my clothes and step in.

I lean back against the back of the tub. From somewhere out on the deck carries in the sound of Puccini. My soul is instantly soothed.

Music has always been my passion. A passion my mother completely dismissed and diminished.

I listen more closely to identify the song. It's from La Bohème–"Sì, mi chiamano Mimì"–an Aria I learned in Performance Study at Smith. I lift my voice to join along, seeking and finding the pleasure of the notes.

The sound reverberates against the bathroom walls, satisfying me, soothing me.

It feels like a return to self.

I belt out the song louder–because you can't half-ass opera. I pour myself into the music like I'm Maria Callas holding center stage, singing my lungs out. It feels good to empty my breath, to move energy this way. Like always, singing trans-forms me. I forget about the rigid constraints my parents and my upbringing imposed on my behavior and my life. When I sing, I exist in oneness. I'm not Dahlia King, socialite and debutante. I simply...am. I'm the song, the music, the words, the wind. I'm a voice and a breath and a soul full of unexpressed emotion.

Lifted and enlivened, I climb out of the tub and dry off, still singing.

I wrap the towel under my armpits and walk out into the bedroom then stop short, the E dying in my throat.

"Don't stop." Antonio reclines in the armchair, his knees spread, his hands resting on the two arms of the chair. He's the picture of relaxed power and authority. Sexy, dominant, far too delicious.

He leans forward. "Please, go on. I've never heard anything so beautiful in my life."

I blink, not believing him at first, but his expression is rapt. His attention fully focused on me. I don't detect any sarcasm or manipulation.

I start up again, but falter, embarrassed. But Antonio remains apparently entranced, so I find my way back to the song. I close my eyes because it's too intense to look at him when I sing, and I think of the romantic story of Mimi and Rodolfo–their bohemian love at first sight.

As I sing, I wonder what it would've been like if I'd met Antonio that way–as a poor seamstress, free to fall in love with another artist. Free to follow my own desires and direction. To express myself creatively. With abandon.

When the aria ends, I open my balled fists and my eyes. Antonio surges to his feet, applauding.

"Bravo!" he practically shouts his praise. "Bravo, *amore*. Nobody told me." He shakes his head, wonder lighting his whiskey-colored eyes.

My foolish heart beats as fast as a hummingbird's. "Told you what?"

"You're incredible." He reaches for both my hands. "How did I not know? I learned everything about you."

A hot flush of pleasure washes over me. I know it's foolish. There's no reason at all to feel flattered–he learned about me to best my father and steal me from my fiance. But I like hearing it, just the same. Or maybe I like having his large hands engulfing my smaller ones. His skin is even warmer than his gaze.

"My mother doesn't like people to know. She thinks it's too bohemian to be an artist. The Kings are supposed to be the *patrons* of the arts."

Antonio cocks his head. "Why would anyone hide a talent so great from the world? It's a travesty."

"Well, I don't know about that." My gaze trips around the room, unsure where to land.

"Don't be modest." He tips my chin up. His look is intent, as if his new mission in life is to champion my singing.

I don't hate it. I know this man tackles everything in life with a ferocity that can't be denied. Knowing he's behind me on something that means so much to me is a gift. It gives me wings.

Not that I plan to pursue a singing career. But just feeling Antonio's support shifts something that was locked inside me. A compartment there was never allowed to be opened has now had its lock sprung and the drawer drawn out.

"Dahlia, you were born to sing. God gave you a gift that can't be denied."

I'm trembling now. Close to tears although I don't know why. It's like Antonio's prying open the recesses of my heart. I feel exposed and raw and vulnerable and yet terribly, painfully hopeful. Like the candle that was extinguished when I was a young girl has just been relit.

"I can't—I can't *pursue* singing or sing in public..."

"You're a Beretta now. You'll do as you please."

More liquid warmth pours into my chest, spreading down my arms and legs.

But I reel myself in. I can't forget that I'm a prisoner on this yacht. This man may be my husband, but he's also my keeper.

I take a step back. "Do as I please? I hardly think so. Am I not your prisoner here?"

I regret the attack because something shutters behind Antonio's eyes.

"You must bend to my will, yes. But no one else's." There's a ring of honoring in the last sentence that again causes my candle wick to relight. As if Antonio would defend me against anyone who tried to stop me from doing something I wanted to do.

For a moment, I have a glimpse of what it's like to have someone in my court—something I've never had before. It makes my knees weak with wonder.

"Come here, *bella*." Antonio grips the edges of my towel and tugs me toward him. The edges come open, and he uses them to pull my body flush against his. He lowers his head slowly, as if giving me time to pull away, but I'm caught in his golden stare, unable to look away, greedy as always for whatever it is he's about to offer.

He slants his lips across mine in a slow, deliberate kiss. His lips are soft. He tastes of expensive champagne.

I open my mouth to him, slide my tongue between his lips. My timid attempt awakens him, and he drops the towel, cradling the back of my head to kiss me deeply. He gives me teeth and tongue and bruising force. Flames lick between my legs, up my center, burning down my resistance. My resolve.

Antonio eases away. "Will you sing for me, beautiful?" His voice is a coaxing soft rumble. It's a tone I haven't heard from him before, and it makes me feel safe and special. Held.

"Yes." The syllable comes easily.

I don't sing for people because my mother didn't like it, but I do know I'm decent. My college professors often gave me the solos in chorus, and I even got the lead in the musical Gigi once. I didn't even tell my parents I was performing, and I used my middle name for the program, so it wouldn't get back to the society pages in New York.

Antonio strokes the side of my cheek with his thumb. I'm naked, but his eyes stay on my face. We remain that way, staring into each other's eyes. I'm sure some exchange of energy is happening, but I don't know what it means. All I know is my heart's pounding, and my lips tingle and buzz from the kiss.

Antonio gently releases me. "You'd better put on your ugliest pajamas, or I might not be able to hold up my end of our bargain."

A puff of surprised laughter comes from my lips. A buoyancy expands in my chest for the first time since my wedding day. No–that's not true–for the first time since I went off to college. That brief period of time when I had some small freedom. But this is different. This is a warm space of lightness and possibility. Of safety and being held.

How ironic that being forced to marry a stranger bent on revenge would create this sense of freedom.

As I take the reprieve he's offered me and turn away to put on a nightgown and panties, I contemplate it.

It's not real freedom.

It must be just the sense of nothing left to lose.

Except that doesn't feel true, either. Because Antonio just gave me a gift, and it's not not the reprieve from sex, which I may have actually given him tonight. It's something else.

A feeling I want to keep.

A new sense of myself–of what I could be outside the boundaries my parents set for me. Of who I am apart from them.

Maybe who I am with Antonio.

I brace against that thought, expecting to feel it thud like my head against the wall, but nothing hits. In fact, the thought only makes me feel lighter.

I cast a nervous glance at my new husband, who has undressed to his boxer shorts and is heading into the bathroom.

For the first time in forever, I don't know what my future holds.

For the first time in forever, I'm actually excited to find out...

# Chapter Seven

*ntonio*

A I wake in the morning when Dahlia makes a tiny adjustment to her position.

She's curled in a ball with her back to me, pretending to still be asleep.

I barely made it through the night without pinning my wife down on the mattress, stripping her of the flimsy nightgown she wore to bed, and stroking every inch of her body. I'm dying to apply my tongue between her legs again and watch her come undone. Nudge those knees apart and find out what it feels like to sink into that wet heat to claim what's mine.

I barely slept, but I wasn't willing to leave my honeymoon bed and sleep elsewhere.

Last night when I heard Dahlia sing, something changed for me. She became more real. I saw the vulnerability of a girl with a passion she hasn't been permitted to pursue. I was knocked over by an unfathomable desire to make every dream she's ever had come true.

But why not? She's my wife. Shouldn't I take care of what belongs to me?

My revenge is already complete. The wedding and the signing over of King Yacht Company was an ending.

What I do with my bride is not part of that.

No, what I–*we*–have now is a beginning.

I could have claimed her last night. I felt the way she responded to my kiss. Saw the wonder of her gaze on my face. But for once in my life, it didn't feel right to press my advantage.

Now, though, I'm kicking myself. I may die of blue balls this very day.

I wrap my fingers around her hip.

She stiffens. She's still afraid of me.

Her bones are small, and my hands are big, so I can grip the entire width of her pelvis. I want to hold it like a handle while I drill–

I draw in a measured breath as my fingers tighten. "I know you're awake, *Principessa*."

The silky fabric of her nightgown doesn't help matters. I pull down the covers to get a better look at it. It's beautiful–a silk shell covered with a gossamer outer layer that slips and slides across her frame.

I love it until I remember–

"You bought this for him." The accusation comes out as a jealous snarl, far more harshly than I intend.

Dahlia rolls to face me. "Of course I did," she snaps.

I work to slow my breath and calm down, but instead, I grow more agitated.

"Were you excited to wear it for him?" I demand. "Did you hope he'd like it?"

It takes me a moment to see through my jealous haze

that there are tears in Dahlia's eyes as she sits up and glares at me. "I did what I was supposed to do."

I rise as well.

She flounces off the bed, yanking the top cover with her to wrap around her shoulders. "I did what was expected of me." She stomps toward the bathroom then stops in the doorway to face me. "That's all I've ever done except for the one moment I took a risk and kissed a dangerous man who let me smoke his cigarette and made my toes curl when he touched me."

She enters the bathroom and slams the door behind her.

I stare after her, stillness creeping through my entire frame, gluing me to the bed.

I digest what she just revealed: I'm her only mistake.

And I made her toes curl.

"Dahlia." Now I'm in motion, headed for the bathroom.

The door is locked, but I use my thumbnail to turn it and open the door.

She faces me, arms folded across her youthful breasts, her jaw thrust forward in defensiveness.

"Come here." I hold out my arms.

She eyes me warily.

"Come here, *Principessa*. That wasn't fair. Of course you bought that for your mayor. You didn't know you wouldn't be marrying him."

To my horror, she blinks and two big tears skate down her cheeks. Her chin juts up. "I didn't buy it for him. I bought it because that's what you're supposed to do. Because that's what my mom said I needed. Are you asking me if I love him? Care about him? Why don't you ask me that?"

I grind my molars. There's a challenge in her voice that I have to meet.

"Do you?" I growl across clenched teeth.

She holds my gaze as she shakes her head. "No." Her voice breaks a little. "So if you thought you were getting revenge on me by breaking my heart, the joke's on you."

Aw, fuck.

I suspected it wasn't a love match, but I thought she was still enamored with the idea of marrying into the powerful political family. That she was a willing participant in the transactional marriage.

Now, just like last night, I see that Dahlia's just a beautiful girl caught in a web of expectations and conventions that she never cared for. That's why she sought me out on the night of her debutante ball. Why she trembled last night when I told her she could sing.

"I'm sorry."

She never stepped into my offered embrace, so I draw her to me now, pulling her head against my chest and kissing the top of it.

She pushes against my chest to lift her face. "What are you sorry for?" She still wears a mulish expression. She resents me like she resents everyone in her life who has told her what to do and expected her to bend to their wishes. I'm no better than her parents. I've given her no choice in her future.

Regret pierces my chest, but I push it away.

My plan has been executed. There's no changing course now. Dahlia's mine, and I won't let her go.

"That your life hasn't been your own."

Her eyes fill with tears again as she searches my face. I cradle her cheek with my palm and stroke my thumb across her soft skin.

"You're not sorry," she tells me. "You just want to be the

one who controls me now." She pushes past me, out of the bathroom, and I let her go because she's absolutely right.

"I don't *want to be* the one who controls you," I tell her back as she faces the dresser to change. "I *am* the one who controls you."

# Chapter Eight

**D**ahlia

I spend the day on the deck in a swimsuit reading my book. The air is warm and balmy. We definitely left New England waters. I'm too proud to ask where we are, since it doesn't really matter. Antonio says he won't let me off until we've consummated the marriage, so I plan to hold out. *For years if I have to.*

That would serve him right.

I eat lunch by myself on the deck. In the late afternoon, I spot land. To my surprise, we drop anchor. I have no idea where we are, but this could be an opportunity to get word to my father. Maybe Shawn, the captain, is already working that plan. I should try to see him again.

I put the bookmark in my novel and stand up from the chaise lounge, trying to come up with a plan.

Antonio strolls to my side. "Put a dress on, darling. I'll take you to dinner."

My heart double pumps with the sudden rush of adrenaline that floods my system. Perfect. This could be my chance to get away.

Well, scratch that. I'm not going to make an escape attempt until I've spoken to my father. I would hate to sign my parents' death warrant by angering Antonio. But if what Shawn told me is true, it sounds like my father is working on a plan to get us free. I need to get word to him about our location at the very least. Even better if I could actually speak to him.

"Fine," I say, as if going to dinner with Antonio is a chore, not an opportunity. I breeze past him and go to the room to get dressed.

I put on a white minidress with a pair of heeled sandals. I might as well work every distraction I have available to me. My legs, tanned and long, look decadent, if I do say so myself.

Antonio's rumble of approval when I emerge shouldn't satisfy me so much, but it does. I drink in his heated gaze, giving my hips an extra swing as I walk. This man makes my body come alive. He thrills me like Jake never could. Like no other man has.

He takes my hand, and we climb down to the speed boat waiting below.

"Where are we?" I ask when we disembark.

"Miami."

Still the U.S.. I can work with that.

"Oh good, I love Cuban food." I pull my hand from his grasp and give my hair a toss as I stride forward.

Two of his men instantly flank me, and I jump, feeling threatened.

"Step back from my wife," Antonio growls.

His use of the word *wife* is no less shocking this time. It's like the man electrocutes me every time he lays claim on me. And I can't say I completely dislike it.

The men give me space.

I wait for Antonio to fall into step beside me again. Given the choice between him or his men, I'll take him. Besides, I need him to think he has me in hand, so I can get away later. Escape to a bathroom and get the use of a phone. Something.

He rests a hand lightly at my lower back, and we walk down the esplanade. "Have you been to Miami before?"

"I haven't," I admit.

"There's a shop here known for its black pearls. Do they interest you?"

I sense Antonio's desire to please me. Perhaps that's why I get stubborn. "No."

He tugs me into one of the shops. "Let's have a look anyway."

A well-dressed man stands behind the case. He inclines his head and greets us. "Good afternoon."

"Good afternoon." I glance at the jewelry in the glass display cases, aware of Antonio's attention on me. The intensity with which he regards my interest. I don't dare look for a phone or accomplice yet.

"Show us those." He points at the one necklace my gaze bounced over—a single giant pearl mounted in white gold on an arty asymmetrical curve.

It's stunning.

Not conservative or predictable.

I would've hated a regular strand of pearls. I've been wearing white pearls my whole life. Every female I know wears white pearls. I could care less about the look or the expense of them.

This piece is different, though.

Antonio points to the case at a matching ring. "Show us the ring, as well."

The shopkeeper rushes to serve him, pulling out both

pieces and putting the necklace on me before I can protest. He holds a mirror up for me to admire.

It's lovely. Rainbows dance and glimmer in the shimmering black-silver orb.

The shopkeeper tries to put the ring on my right hand, but Antonio takes it off, removes the engagement and wedding ring Jake bought, and slides it in place there instead.

I hate that it fits me perfectly because I don't want to love it so much. Nor do I want to feel gratified that he wants to replace that ring. I wanted to keep hanging onto that offense and use it to stroke my defenses against him.

"We'll take them both. And those earrings." Antonio points to a pair of two-inch long drop earrings with giant black pearls on the ends of a single white gold shaft.

He shells out an ungodly amount of money, and I wear the set out of the shop.

When we get outside, he holds my jaw and turns my head from side to side, inspecting me the way he did in the limo on our wedding day. "They suit you. Classy but different from the rest. Far more unique than the others."

I fight the warmth his words produce. Fight it with all the resistance I can muster. "Am I supposed to thank you?"

He releases my jaw. "No. You wearing them is thanks enough."

I turn those words over and around in my head, wondering what they mean. Why would he care if I wear his gift or not. What he truly wants with me.

Because it feels like it's changed.

He's not just out for revenge. If that were the case, he wouldn't care if I wore his ring. He wouldn't buy me a new ring.

No, Antonio is trying to please me.

And as much as I hate to admit it...I'm pleased.

Which changes nothing with regard to my plan to make contact with my father tonight.

*  *  *

*Antonio*

A strange thing has happened.

I simply like to be in the presence of my wife. Yes, she's easy on the eyes, but it's more than that. I like to hear her voice, even when it's tight and defensive. I like to watch her expressions. I like seeing that while she tries to hide her feelings, she's attracted to me. Enjoys my attention.

If I let her win a few rounds, she just might drop her defenses again. We might have a chance of an actual marriage. It's not what I wanted–not what I expected–at least not consciously. But this woman has been at the center of my revenge plan from the beginning. She was the trigger. The girl I was told I wasn't good enough for and didn't deserve.

The one who became a symbol of everything I had to be angry for. Except she was a shimmering, shiny symbol. Something I had to attain, capture, and keep.

The sensual, enigmatic beauty of the ball.

The prize.

My prize. What I actually deserved, that evening of her ball and now.

No, maybe not now. Because I haven't earned her affection yet. I fought unfairly, and I won.

Now it may be time to actually court my wife. To find out what makes her tick. How to make her smile, laugh, sing.

And–ah God–her voice! Like an angel's.

After hearing her sing last night, I feel I've glimpsed the real Dahlia. The vulnerable, talented artist who was never allowed to express her gifts.

It made me want to wring her parents' necks.

And now I'm determined to make sure she gets to do everything she dreamed of doing.

Which is why I choose a festive open-air restaurant with a lively band singing contemporary English pop music instead of the more expensive fine dining Dahlia would be accustomed to.

American tourists sit under palapas, sucking down fruity cocktails.

I watch as curiosity overtakes Dahlia's tension. She watches the band and the happy, drunken tourists around us as our waiter takes our drink order.

She sucks down a banana daiquiri, and I order her another. Her mood lightens considerably. While we eat a simple but delicious fish dinner, she rolls her shoulders a little then nods her head to the music, smiling at the band.

"They're good, no?" I ask.

"So good."

"Do you sing this kind of music? Or only opera?"

"I love this kind of music. I sing everything. If I could've done anything, I would've been a Broadway musical star."

My heart.

She has the talent for it, too. What a shame her parents didn't support her dreams.

When she excuses herself to the restroom after dinner, I send one of my men to keep an eye on her, and I speak to the lead singer.

People are up dancing now, some sloppy drunk, others with more class. I take Dahlia's hand when she returns and lead her to the dance floor. Her heart beats quickly at her throat.

She's excited. To dance with me?

It occurs to me this girl has probably lived her life in a deficit of fun. Of letting loose. Letting go. We dance a few songs, and I order her another drink but keep her on the dance floor. We dance until her face is flushed and her eyes are bright.

Then I lead her up onto the stage and tell the lead singer she's going to perform with them.

"What? No!" Dahlia tries to pivot and retreat, but I gently nudge her forward.

"She's an incredible singer," I explain. "Tell them what to play, *bella*, and they'll play it." I slipped the lead singer a tip earlier to make sure he treats her right.

"Um..." Dahlia flicks a glance at me, and I wink. "Can you play 'Be My Baby'?"

The band strikes up the music, and Dahlia takes the microphone that the lead singer offers her. She sings.

Ten songs later, the place is rocking, and Dahlia's the new star. I maintain a position below the stage, just in front of her. Her biggest fan and her keeper.

I ensure she's supplied with water and daiquiris, and I drink in her talent. Her presence. Her poise. Her charisma.

She could be a star. Should already be one.

She's incredible.

When she starts to slur and sway on her feet, I catch her hand and tug her off the stage and into my arms in a honeymoon carry.

"Let's go back to the yacht, *amore*."

She loops her arms around my neck and kisses my temple. "That was fun."

"Was it?"

"Thank you."

She sounds sincere, and it does something funny to my chest. Twists and tugs it.

"I take care of what's mine," I tell her.

She bites my ear. "So I'm yours?" She slides her tongue around the shell of my ear.

My dick gets rock hard.

"You're definitely mine."

If I were a real gentleman, I would not take advantage of her alcohol and fun-induced affection.

But I'm not a gentleman, and she's my wife.

I've been blue-balled for three days now. I am dastardly enough to press my advantage. If I can seduce her now and gain her consent, nothing will stop me from fully claiming my wife.

"Why do you even want me?" she asks drunkenly. "I'm the daughter of your enemy. Shouldn't you be repulsed by me?"

"Repulsed?" I give a mirthless laugh. "Hardly." I carry her into the tender and settle her on my lap for the short boat ride to the yacht. "You forget how I made him my enemy."

Her breasts are at eye level. I open my mouth and bite through the fabric of her dress.

She mewls and squirms on my lap. I narrow my bite and zero in on her nipple, nipping it through her clothing.

"You were attracted to me." She says it with a tinge of wonder, like it hadn't occurred to her.

I guess I'd forgotten it myself–the aftermath had blotted out the original experience. My life ruined over a kiss and a second-base grope.

"Mmm hmm." I stroke my thumb along her throat. "You're a beautiful woman. New York aristocracy. You should have been out of reach for a guy like me, but there you were, coming after me like you saw something you wanted."

Dahlia pivots on my lap and shocks me by straddling my waist. I doubt it's so she can grind over me–she probably just wants to look at my face, but that doesn't stop me from yanking her core right over my hardened cock.

She instantly starts rocking on it. I don't think she even knows what she's doing, but her body understands exactly what's going on.

"I *did* want you," she confesses. "There was something powerful about you, even then."

"Even when I was just the waiter at your ball?" I shouldn't jab at her. Not when her tits are in my face and her hot core is grinding over my dick.

She kisses me. It's a sloppy, excited kiss and her fervor makes me forget everything but the feel of her body against mine. The need to give her pleasure and get my pleasure in return. I catch the side of her face and kiss her back, sweeping my tongue into her mouth, taking over.

She rocks her sweet ass, undulating over my lap. I curl my fingers around one of her cheeks and help her find a rhythm. By the time the boat reaches the yacht, she's breathless and hot.

I waste no time lifting her to the ladder to climb aboard.

She's weaving toward our room when I catch up with her and sweep her back into my arms to carry her the rest of the way. I kick the door closed and set her on her feet, then unzip her dress as I kiss the fuck out of her swollen lips.

She makes little moany sounds into my mouth, her hands sliding over my chest. She works open one of the buttons on my shirt. I tug her dress up over her head.

"You didn't forget me." I don't know why I'm asking.

Why it seems important to know that she didn't kiss every fucking waiter at every fucking ball she attended growing up.

"I never forgot."

I unhook her bra, then tug the straps down until it falls down her arms and onto the floor. "Did you want more than you got that night?" I lightly brush the pad of my thumb over her erect nipple. One hand still has hold of her nape to angle her face up for my kisses. I don't give her a chance to go cold or get nervous.

"Yes," she breathes.

"What would you have given me, if I'd pushed?" I palm her breast and squeeze as I back her toward the bed.

She whimpers her excitement.

"Hmm?" I move to grab her ass now.

"I-I don't know." She's unbuttoned half the buttons on my shirt now. I yank it off, popping the rest of them. Her fingernails scrape across my hairy chest.

I push her onto the bed, falling on top of her. She parts her thighs, allowing me to rub the bulge of my cock in the notch between her legs. She moans in response to the sensation.

"Would you have let me touch you here?" I slide my hand between our bodies, into her panties, my fingertip parting her.

She cries out at the sensation the moment I touch her clit.

Her thighs lift and squeeze around my hips, pulling me against her. "God, yes!"

I chuckle, not sure if the yes is for what I'm doing now or what she would've let me do then. It doesn't matter. I press against her clit and rub a slow circle. Her skin is flushed, her eyelids flutter as her hands coast up and down my shoulders.

I slide my index finger lower and curl it inside her. She moans softly, her pretty mouth falling open and staying that way.

I trail kisses along her jaw, then down her neck.

"I fantasized about you afterward."

Aw, fuck. I can't believe it.

"Yeah? What did I do in those fantasies?" I add a second finger, stretching her tight entrance to ready her for me. "This?"

She shakes her head. "Yes. But this is better. I had no idea."

I gently pump my fingers inside her. "You didn't know it would feel so good?"

She catches her lower lip between her teeth and shakes her head. "No." The syllable sounds desperate, like she's already nearing orgasm.

I don't want her to come without me this time, though. I'm desperate to come with her, to bring us to that place simultaneously.

I unzip my pants and free my erection.

Dahlia sits up on her elbows and stares at it. She doesn't look afraid. More...fascinated.

"You've never felt anything so good as this," I promise her, dragging the head through her juices. "You wanna watch?" I grab a pillow and shove it beneath her shoulders and head, so she doesn't have to strain her neck. "You can watch me fuck you."

I work my cock between her legs, taking my time, using her natural lubrication to get her to stretch and open for me.

She tenses when I press forward, so I ease back.

"Here." I take her hand and wrap it around the base of my cock. "You control it."

Her gaze flies to my face, then back to my cock.

"Put it inside you, Princess."

She tugs gently, and I follow, pressing in at her pace, easing back when she directs me that way. Easily, organically, I get all the way in, her tight channel open and slick for me.

The victory I feel isn't over consummating the marriage or getting my revenge fuck.

It's the trust between us right now. The intimacy. The sense of the two of us being on the same team. I don't own Dahlia in this moment; she owns me. I would do anything to make sure this experience is good for her.

I wrap an arm behind her back and roll us over, so she's on top. "Straddle me," I murmur.

She obeys, pushing on my chest to rise and ride me. I grip her hips to show her how to move, then release my hold and give her ass a pat. "You do it. Show me what feels good to you."

I see the confusion flit over her face. "To me?"

I nod, showing her again. "How do you like it? Can you pleasure yourself this way?"

"Can I...?" She catches that lip again as she starts to grind over me. "Oh!" Her expression of pleasured surprise steals my breath. Her hands drop to my shoulders, and she increases her speed. "*Oh.*" She shifts her hands to the headboard and uses it to push and pull her body over mine. Her movements grow faster and faster, her breath turns to wild panting.

I'll bet I could make her come with one brush of her clit, but I shake my head. "Not yet, *Principessa.*"

She abruptly stops, staring at me with wide eyes like she's done something wrong.

"I want to come with you this time."

I flip her back over on her back. "You gonna come with me?"

She locks gazes with me and nods.

"Good girl." I rock into her, slowly at first. She's sopping wet now, making it easy to glide in and out. "You're so wet, baby. You liked riding my cock, didn't you?"

"Antonio."

The sound of my name on her lips does wild things to my heart. Once more, I belong to her. Want to do everything in my power to hear my name gasped from her throat every fucking day of my life.

I pick up speed, and she starts to chant my name.

This.

This is what I've been missing my whole life.

I've had women. Lots of them. But there's something different about this time. Dahlia's my wife. And not as a symbol, as a conquest. This isn't about me bedding the society darling.

Fuck.

Was all this revenge just about getting the girl?

Had there been something special in that kiss? That meeting?

Were we two souls destined to collide in this lifetime? Did I recognize her then?

I think I did.

With that realization, I lose all control, plowing into her hard, forgetting to be careful with her. I grip the headboard and slam in, again and again, until my balls pump.

I shout as I come and Dahlia wraps her legs around my back, holding me against her. I'm blinded, seeing only fireworks on a black backdrop for a moment as I release and release inside her.

"Dahlia." I remember her, shocked back to reality by the realization that I've been rough with her–terribly rough for an untouched virgin.

Her eyes are squeezed shut.

I reach between us and rub her clit, and her muscles spasm around my cock.

She cries out, arching against me. "Oh my God!"

"That's it, *Principessa*. You come, too."

"Oh God." She continues to clench and squeeze my cock, drawing another release from me. "So good."

Thank fuck.

I roll us to our sides and wrap her in my arms, kissing her forehead, her nose, her lips. "Was that good, sweet girl?"

"Mmm hmm."

I stroke her back, savoring the feel of her soft skin, the way she melts against me and lets me hold her.

For the first time in years, something in me quiets.

It rests.

Dahlia's mine. Maybe not in heart, yet, but in body.

The rest will come.

# Chapter Nine

D*ahlia*

I wake still snuggled in the circle of Antonio's arms. I'm warm and sated. Sore but in a good way.

When I move, Antonio's arms tighten around me, and he kisses the back of my head.

I didn't mean to have sex with him.

Oh, who am I kidding? I wanted it. I have wanted it ever since the night of my debutante ball. Every time I imagined sex, it was with him.

And it was so much better than I ever imagined. So satisfying. So addictive.

I definitely want more.

But the part I never even contemplated was this.

Being held. Stroked. Murmured to between soft kisses.

Antonio's affection terrifies me. It feels so good. Exactly what I've needed my whole life. And now that I've known this kind of attention, I never want to lose it.

Last night when I went to the bathroom, I was able to slip a message to the restaurant host. I promised him my father would reward him handsomely if he called the number and told him I was there.

Whether that will actually happen or not, I can't be sure, but the thought of it now turns my stomach to knots.

Maybe he won't call. He probably threw the paper out, rolling his eyes about the stupid American.

I hope.

This morning the idea of my father showing up to rescue me makes me queasy. Especially because I know that would mean him doing something terrible to Antonio.

It feels foolhardy to believe that the act of sex somehow changed us, but it has. Or maybe it wasn't the sex. Maybe the sex was the result of the thing that changed between us. Antonio made me feel special and loved last night. The way he watched me as I sang filled me. Filled up a crack and crevice in my tattered soul. Every single time I was rejected for being myself growing up. Every time I was not allowed to have my own feelings, control my own life, have my own desires. All of those fissures and caverns and crevices were filled simply with Antonio's admiring gaze.

That he accepted me for what I am and nurtured the rejected parts of me–the wild, rebellious side, the artist who yearned to perform–somehow changed me. I feel more whole today than I've felt maybe ever. Like the splintered, shattered parts of me have been glued back together.

And then there was the sex. I loved it. Not just how it felt in my body, but watching what happened to Antonio when he found his release. I loved seeing him out of control, desperate and needy. And then feeling his immense gratitude afterward.

So yes, everything has changed between us. We are not the same two people who stepped off *The Honeymoon* yesterday.

I could be pregnant with Antonio's child already. That thought, more than any other, slices a streak of terror through me.

How will this all end? If my father is coming for me and Antonio is the father of my child—where does that leave me? I'm Antonio's wife now. If I have his child, I should stay with him.

I can't deny the hint of satisfaction that idea brings me. That circumstances might force me to stay with Antonio and raise a child together. Would he be a good father? Better than mine? I saw something last night that tells me that he would be. An indulgence of me. A nurturing. And the way he let me take charge for my first time in bed. He didn't force himself on me. He didn't even ask if I was okay. He just made sure that I was. He knew exactly what to do to ensure it worked for me. And I love him for that.

Oh God, did I just think the word *love*? I can't love Antonio! He's my captor. My father's enemy.

But what if we're really a mad version of *Romeo and Juliet*? Two lovers from feuding families destined to be together.

Antonio nibbles on my neck.

I didn't brush my teeth last night, and my mouth is filled with cotton. I shove the covers away from my legs and try to swing them off the bed. Antonio catches me and drags me back into the bed.

"Where do you think you're going?" He pins me down, hovering over me to give me a kiss.

I turn my face away. "I have bad breath!"

"I don't care."

He clearly doesn't because he kisses me fully, his tongue delving between my lips, showing me that our mouths are one. Our breath, shared. When he pulls back, he reaches for a glass of water beside the bed, lifts my head from the mattress and puts it to my lips.

"How are you this morning?"

I drink down the entire glass of water and he chuckles. "A little hungover? I'd hoped I kept you up long enough last night for it to wear off."

My body heats at the reminder of how he kept me up. "You did. I mean, I'm good. Totally fine. I just need to brush my teeth."

"Okay, I guess that's allowed." His smile reveals dimples I haven't seen enough of. He releases me. "But come right back to bed."

I climb out, surprised at how unembarrassed I am by my full nudity. I sense Antonio admiring my body, and it heats me from the inside out. He wants me to come back to bed. What does he have in mind? I'm not sure I can face him naked again in the light of day without alcohol.

Except that's not true. As I use the toilet and brush my teeth, my heart hammers with anticipation. I can't wait to climb back in that bed and feel his hands on my skin again. It's like my body knows where it belongs, and it's next to his.

I emerge from the bathroom to find him propped up in the bed, looking like a Roman god. He opens the covers and holds his arms out to me. "Come here."

When I comply, he pulls me up against him and strokes his hand down my side. "Are you sore, *Principessa*?" His fingers trail between my thighs—a light touch that doesn't quite reach the apex.

"A little," I say.

He finds the evidence of his dried essence on my inner thighs and rumbles his approval. "You didn't wash me off."

I flush. Was I supposed to? These are the things I know nothing about.

"I like it. Never wash me off," he commands. "It's a new rule."

"I don't follow your rules." I say it lightly–there's no venom behind the words. I just want him to know I'm going to keep pushing back. I may have let him consummate the marriage, but that doesn't mean he's in charge of me or that I've conceded to this marriage.

The corners of his lips lift. "That's because you enjoy the consequences of your disobedience. He rolls me to my back and climbs over me, backing up until his head is in line with my pelvis.

My core squeezes in anticipation.

"Open your thighs, Dahlia. This time it will be a reward."

You don't have to tell me twice. I let my knees fall open and Antonio lowers his head between my legs.

My belly shivers in an inhale. Antonio drags his tongue along my slit, parting me.

"Oh, *God*." It feels so good.

Even better than it did the last time. It's like the more Antonio touches me, the more he pleasures me, the more receptive my body becomes. I'm primed for him now, ready to climax at the slightest provocation.

And provoke, he does.

Antonio swirls his tongue around my clit, traces everywhere. He sucks and teases, uses his teeth on the little nubbin of my clit.

I gasp, my pelvis jacking up off the mattress at the delicious sensation.

"You like that, *bella*?"

"Uhn." I let out an unintelligible syllable, somewhere between a groan and a cry. It feels so good. I want it all. Everything he did to me last night and more.

He palms my ass, lifts my pelvis to angle me more toward his mouth. His entire mouth covers my sex as he laps and penetrates me with his clever tongue.

I wrap my fingers in his hair and tug, growing desperate.

"You need to come, baby?" He slides a finger inside me.

I squirm down on his finger. My entrance is tender, but I don't care. The sensation is incredible. Needed. I'm wet and slick, and his finger feels too small.

"I want..."

"What do you want, *Principessa*?"

"I want you."

Antonio's grin is wicked. "Say it. Say, *I need your cock, Antonio*."

"I need your cock, Antonio."

That's all it takes. In a flash, my husband is above me, lining his member up with my entrance. The satisfaction when he pushes in cannot be named. Cannot be described.

It's just that sense of *rightness*. Of our bodies belonging together.

I reach for his shoulders, hanging on as he slowly arcs in and out, watching my face the entire time.

Remembering how marvelous it was to watch him come undone last night, I moan my approval. Try to get him to stop tracking me and lose himself.

Antonio cages my throat, using his grip to hold me in place as he pushes in with more force.

It hurts but in a good way. A satisfying way. Definitely an *I-want-more* way.

I grow louder, not for Antonio's benefit now, but because I'm in the throes, myself. It feels so good to have him moving inside me, to match my pleasure to his.

Antonio's breath grows ragged, his face grows slack above me. "Dahlia," he growls.

That's all it takes for me. Just the sound of my name in his deep voice makes me come. I seize up around him, hooking my ankles behind his back to draw him in.

"Wait...*fuck*," he pants, still plowing into me. *"Now."* He shoves in and stays, filling me with his hot seed.

My body understands his command because the orgasm that rolls through me is like nothing I've experienced before. My internal muscles contract and release around him, my inner thighs squeeze tight around his hips. I bite his neck, suck his earlobe, gasp and cry out and whimper as our bodies find completion together.

"Oh, baby." Antonio pants into my neck. He lifts his head and cages my jaw in that dominant way of his. "You were incredible. So good, baby. Are you all right?"

I nod in his grip.

"Was I too rough? I know you're still getting used to me."

"I liked it."

His smile makes butterflies swirl in my belly. "Of course you did." He says it with such pride that I crack open, and something that's been locked up and caged forever rolls free. He lowers his head and kisses me hard, and I receive him, glorying in this new bond we've forged–whatever it may be.

But I don't get a chance to explore it further because at that moment, the door explodes inward and two men dressed in camo and carrying machine guns barge into the room.

# Chapter Ten

*A*ntonio

I throw my body in front of Dahlia's to protect her from the intruders at the same time I reach for my gun beside the bed.

"Don't shoot!" A voice shouts from above deck. "My daughter's in there!"

Aw, *fuck*.

Benedict King must want to die.

I point the gun back and forth between the two men. They must be mercenaries–ex-US military types. "Shoot me, and you'll risk her."

"Dahlia, get away from him!" one of the men growls.

The sound of her name on his lips is all it takes to make me go off. I shoot him then the other guy in less than one second.

Dahlia screams at the top of her lungs.

I leap up from the bed and run to the door.

"Dahlia!" Her father calls from out on the deck.

"Don't shoot!" she screams back.

I'm not sure if she's pleading with me or him.

I storm out and up the stairs to the deck and immediately draw fire from the sun deck. I duck back into the corridor, peering up in the direction it came.

I see one of my men dangling from the railing, blood pouring from his head. Another of my soldiers lies on the deck.

*Fanculo.*

I aim my pistol toward the sun deck and slowly shift my weight out until I'm far enough to take aim. A bullet strikes the wall directly beside my head, but mine finds home in another merc.

I hear shouts in Italian and more gunfire. Some of my men are still alive, then.

"Dahlia?"

I spot Benedict hiding behind two of his mercs. He has a gun in his hand but holds it awkwardly. He'll probably shoot his own foot before he fires on me. I take down the two men guarding him.

"No!" Dahlia screams. She's thrown on a robe and is coming up the stairs behind me.

"Get back in the cabin," I snarl. "It's not safe out here."

"Dahlia!"

My attention is drawn away from Benedict by three of his men rounding the corner. I shield Dahlia's body and take them out.

Before I know it, Dahlia has darted past me and is running for her father. "Daddy! You got my message!"

The ship spins. Or maybe I'm spinning. Something is fucking spinning.

Dahlia sent a message to her father last night. That's how he found us here.

Betrayal stabs deep in my heart, igniting my old rage.

My old need for revenge. Yes, I'm a brute, a true monster, but the Kings are what made me this way.

I lift my pistol and point it right at Benedict's head. I'm an excellent shot. Not one of my bullets has missed its mark thus far. One twitch of my finger, and he would be dead.

He's hustling Dahlia to the rail and pointing over the side. There must be a motor boat pulled alongside ours. How it got close without my men spotting it is unfathomable to me.

I follow them with my gun arm extended, Benedict's head clearly in my sight.

My wife—the woman I just made scream with pleasure—has one leg over the railing. She glances back at me, and her eyes round with terror. "No!" her scream rings with so much horror that I draw my hand up, pointing toward the sky instead of her father. "Please, Antonio—"

She doesn't get to finish the plea because her father fires wildly at me.

I've reached them by now.

Benedict shoves Dahlia off the rail, and we both stand there a moment, peering off the side at her flailing body plummeting down.

I'm holding my breath, afraid she might crack her head on the boat below, but she misses it, plunging into the water.

I slam my hand down on Benedict's wrist, causing him to lose grip on the pistol. It fires wildly as it falls to the deck and slides away from us. I press my gun to his temple.

"Antonio!"

The sound of my name on my wife's lips makes something deep inside of me shudder with recognition. Despite her betrayal, it's all still there—my desire to please her. To make her happy.

I tear my glance away from her father to peer over the

rail. She's swimming beside the boat, one arm tossed over the side to steady herself.

She catches my gaze. "Antonio, no. *Please.*"

She's begging me.

As I desired.

As I predicted.

But not the reason I'd hoped.

Fanculo.

I jab the pistol into Benedict's flesh. "Jump," I snarl.

He scrambles to comply.

"Jump," I repeat. "If I see you again, you're a dead man."

He topples sloppily over the side, hitting a limb on the lower railing as he goes, likely breaking his arm.

I look back at my wife. She hasn't moved to climb in the boat. She's still staring up at me, stricken.

What? What is it?

What does she want from me?

I aim my pistol at her father, who is already climbing in the boat. He yanks the rope free from The Honeymoon's ladder and starts the engine of the boat as Dahlia climbs in.

And then they're gone.

My revenge has been undone.

It's gone flat.

And I don't even care.

The rage in me is quiet.

In fact, I feel nothing at all.

I'm totally blank. Empty. As dead as the bloody bodies strewn across the slick deck.

It's over.

My revenge plan, my marriage, my plans for the future. I just conceded everything to a little blonde debutante who sings like a bird.

* * *

*Dahlia*

My father paces back and forth, a blanket from the bed draped around his shoulders. We're at a hotel in Miami, and he is on the phone with Senator Reese, Jake's father, talking about the logistics and illegality of getting U.S. Marines down here to take Antonio out.

I go into the bathroom and step into the shower, my wet clothing still on. I stand under the spray for a long time, then I sit down on the tile floor and hold my head in my hands.

What have I done?

What has my father done?

And Antonio?

Men died today over this feud. I should be applauding my father's new plan, but I can't. I'm just sick over all of it.

None of this had to happen, starting with my father condemning Antonio to prison for a crime he didn't commit.

I guess we truly are Romeo and Juliet, and this all ends in tragedy.

The image of Antonio's body being one of the many corpses we left on that yacht today makes me choke with a sob. The numbness cracks, and I break down–full-on, ugly crying.

How would I feel if Antonio had been killed today? It would have been all my fault. I'm the one who delivered the message to my father about where to find us. I saw the shock of betrayal in Antonio's expression when he realized what I'd done, and it makes my stomach knot and twist.

Does he hate me now, too?

The thought leaves me broken. Bereft. I didn't even

want to leave the yacht when I jumped over the side. I wanted to run back to Antonio's bed and crawl back in his arms.

Oh, God. Was it only this morning that we made love? It feels like years ago. Centuries.

Lifetimes have passed since he kissed me.

I scrub my hands over my cheeks, my tears mixed with the shower water.

What now?

Am I going to let them plot Antonio's murder?

My hand finds my belly. It's unlikely, but possible that I could be pregnant right now with his child. Am I going to allow my father to kill my husband?

I struggle to my feet and rip my wet robe from my body. I have to stop this madness.

It has to stop here.

Antonio belongs to me now as much as he believes I belong to him.

We're married.

And that's when I realize something else. Perhaps the most important thing of all: Antonio cares about me.

He let my father go.

It wasn't because he's not a killer–he clearly is. I watched him shoot at least four men today. He hates my father–spent years of his life plotting his revenge against him.

And yet today he let him go.

I can only surmise it's because I asked.

Because he cares for me. He hasn't said so. He's called me beautiful, made me feel beautiful, but he hasn't said I mean anything to him other than as a conquest.

But if I were just a conquest, he wouldn't spare my

father. Especially not after realizing I'd betrayed him and wanted to escape.

And for the record—I didn't want to.

I'd do anything if I could back in time and not deliver that message to the restaurant host last night.

To still be with Antonio on the yacht. Or off the yacht, for that matter. Where would he have brought me to live? What would our life have looked like?

All those questions make my heart strain, as if pulled long and twisted.

I turn off the water and towel off, then wrap up in a fluffy hotel robe and step out into the suite to confront my father.

"You have to let Antonio go."

"It's too late." My father shakes his head. "The FBI is on their way to arrest Antonio right now. With the bodycount he left today, he'll never see the light of day again."

# Chapter Eleven

*Antonio*

I light a match and flick it into the pool of gasoline and The Honeymoon bursts into furious flames.

I watch for a few moments.

I don't know what I hope for—some glimmer of satisfaction at ruining Benedict's beautiful vessel?

Instead, I feel nothing but the gnawing emptiness that's been with me since the moment Dahlia jumped over the side.

My men and I motor away from the unanchored yacht, now a Norse burial ship, carrying the dead across the rainbow bridge, or wherever the fuck they supposedly go.

I lost three. We took out a dozen of theirs.

I should be satisfied that the battle was won, but all I taste is the ash in my mouth.

"Where to?" Leo, my soldier behind the wheel, asks.

I shake my head.

"You don't know, boss? Or you don't care?"

"Head to Miami, you idiot," Il Greco, my capo, mutters.

"We're in a fucking motorboat. It's not like we can sail to Australia."

"Shut up." I just need to think. To figure out my next move. I always have the next move. I'm the fucking king of strategy.

Except right now, my mind is completely blank.

I don't care about the next move.

I don't care about anything at all.

It's no longer about revenge. I realize, suddenly, that it never was. It was about that girl in the closet who I felt unworthy of.

All this work was actually to bring myself up to Dahlia's level. To make myself worthy of her.

And I just blew it all by showing her what I really am.

A monster.

# Chapter Twelve

*Antonio*

I stand on the balcony of my Manhattan apartment and look down.

Dahlia's in this city, not that I've seen her.

But illogically, her presence here is what drew me back. I needed to breathe the same air she breathes. Walk the same streets.

Every cell in my body aches for her. It seems incredible that I only had her in my bed four short nights because I seem to remember every single freckle on her skin, every curve of her flesh. I remember how silky her hair is, the way her mouth parts when she's close to coming.

And the music.

It haunts me all day and night.

I hear her voice singing Puccini. I remember the joy on her face when she was on that stage in Miami, singing pop songs and dancing with abandon.

"Boss, you gotta see this." Il Greco comes out on the balcony and shoves a newspaper in my face. It's the society pages of the Manhattan Times, and the bold headline reads, "Yacht King Heiress Spills About Her Marriage."

I thrust it back at him. "I don't want to read it."

"No. Really, Antonio. You need to read it."

My lip curls in a snarl, but I snatch the paper back and snap it open. What kind of fuckery do I have to strategize around now?

In the days I've been back, I've expected some kind of assault from King. I expected the FBI or more mercs. I bolstered security on the King Yacht operations and my private residence, but nothing has come.

Now, it seems they're fighting with public opinion.

What a laugh—as if a brute like me gives a fuck what people think of him. I'm a Beretta. My reputation was tarnished the day I was born.

*King Yacht heiress Dahlia King reveals all about the man she has loved since she was fifteen.* My eyes slow as the words jumble and rearrange themselves on the page.

What is this?

I reread the pull quote then start again at the beginning.

*Dahlia Beretta (King), daughter of Benedict and Barbara King, gave an exclusive interview to the Times this week to explain her last-minute change in groom at her wedding. Last week, the heiress was expected to marry New York City Mayor Jake Reese in a very large and public wedding spectacle in Cape Cod, yet guests were stunned when the mayor did not appear at the altar.*

*Rather, Antonio Beretta of New Jersey, a man with a criminal record and ties to the mafia stood at the altar and claimed the bride. Beretta also became the sole shareholder of the entire King Yacht enterprise that day.*

*Speculation over the past two weeks has been that the*

*bride and her father may have been coerced, but the truth is actually even more spectacular of a story.*

*According to Mrs. Beretta, she and Antonio have been in love since she met him as a teenager. Her father did not approve and alleged the young man stole from him while working as a caterer at Mrs. Beretta's debutante ball.*

*Beretta was later sentenced to three years in prison for the crime, which Mrs. Beretta maintains he did not commit and was fabricated by her father to keep the two apart.*

*The wedding swap was an elaborate plan worked up by the couple to be able to fully celebrate their partnership and matrimony with all of New York's society as witnesses. Mrs. Beretta said it was important to her that society see and recognize the union, which would have been snubbed had it been previously announced.*

I stop reading and scrub a hand across my face.

What does this mean? What is Dahlia up to?

It's a trap of some sort.

Except my traitorous heart has grown warm and full.

What if it's not a trap? What if this is Dahlia's attempt to save me? Perhaps from her father, perhaps from the law.

I'm moving before the thought has fully formed in my mind.

I have to find her. To see her.

Dahlia cares about me.

Maybe, she even loves me, as the article claims.

And if that's true, then every second I'm not with her is wasted.

I jog to the door and get in my new 1964 convertible Corvette.

Dahlia Beretta belongs to me, and I'm going to go and get her. I park on the street beneath her parents' luxury skyrise apartment on Central Park.

"Antonio Beretta here to see my wife, Dahlia."

The doorman is obviously prepared for me. His eyes dart around nervously, but he holds his ground.

"I'm sorry, Mr. Beretta, but I've been instructed to ask you to leave."

I shake my head. "I'm not leaving without my wife."

The guy swallows. He's scared as shit of me. Sweat trickles down his brow. "Should I call the police, sir?"

"Call Dahlia. Tell her I'm here."

"I'm sorry, sir. I have my instructions."

"*Now.*"

The guy jumps but shakes his head. "I-I'm calling the cops."

*Fanculo.*

I'm tempted to use intimidation, but I check my aggression. I feel quite certain Dahlia wouldn't want me to rough up her parent's doorman.

"Fine."

I park my car on the opposite side of the street and lean my ass against the car door. I fold my arms across my chest and settle in to watch the entrance. Sooner or later, some member of the King family will come out that door, and I will be here to talk to them.

Of course, the sky opens up and begins to pour rain down on me.

I put the top up on the car but don't change my position.

I don't care if I have to wait for five days in the fucking rain.

I'm not leaving here until I see my wife.

\* \* \*

*Dahlia*

"You ruined this family!" My mother screams at me. She's been crying all morning, ever since the article came out in the *Manhattan Times* society pages.

I was able to shut down or at least stall my father's plan to send the FBI after Antonio with my promise to go public with the whole story if he did.

He whisked us back to Manhattan, and I've been a prisoner here ever since. I called Bea to come and get me, but the doorman refused to let her in. My father has security guards stationed outside our door–ostensibly for our protection, but when I tried to go out, they wouldn't let me.

That's why I called the reporter. I realized it was a way to protect Antonio in the future. Now, anything that happens to him will be examined by the public, and hopefully, the law, with the lens of the story I wove about star-crossed lovers kept apart. Another *West Side Story*. I kept out the part about Antonio ruining my father financially and the bloodbath on *The Honeymoon*.

"*I'm* not the one who ruined it." My voice holds all the censure I have for my father and his behavior. He's the one who mistreated Antonio. The one who was cocky or foolish enough to lose his entire fortune to the man, and the man who somehow still thinks he has any say in my life or how I live it.

I'm no longer beholden to my parents. The fetters of obligation and obedience are finally gone. I may have thought I was an adult before my wedding day, but I was still a child, acting for them.

Now, I'm a woman. A woman with power she can wield all on her own, simply with a call to a reporter.

"I'm not the one who started a war with the Beretta

Crime Family and thinks he can win it. But I *am* the one who can put an end to it."

"You put an end to *us*. To everything we had. You were going to be a *president's wife*," my mother shrieks. She's at the wet bar, pouring herself a drink, even though it's barely after noon. Outside, the sky is charcoal grey, and pouring rain.

"We have nothing," I remind her. "My husband already took it all."

My mother whirls, her mouth open in shock at my use of the words *my husband*. "Is that what this is about? You care about this man?" Before I can answer, she draws herself up into a rant. "You don't care about him! Those were lies you told the newspaper. Desperate lies designed to ruin us. You just want your revenge because you had no say in your marriage."

"Ah." I fold my arms across my chest. "There it is. You finally admit it. You've been trying to sugarcoat your choices for my life all these years, but that's the reality. I was a prisoner in a gilded cage. Raised only to do your bidding and fulfill the destiny you wish you'd had!"

"Enough." My father emerges from his office in yesterday's clothes. His hair is tousled, and there's an alcohol stain on his shirt. Like my mother, he's day drinking. "We need to pull together as a family now. We're all we have."

I let out a scoff.

The last thing I want to do is pull together with this family.

Out on the street, someone is blasting Puccini–the same damn song I sang for Antonio.

My heart feels as if it will rip from my chest.

The story I told the reporter wasn't a lie. I have loved that man since the day I met him. Maybe I didn't know him, but my soul recognized his. We were destined for each other. I feel certain of it.

Nothing else would explain this connection I've felt with him from the beginning. The flutters of excitement every time I'm in his presence, the sense of trust I feel without there being any basis for it.

I almost got him killed by trying to "pull together" with my parents. What would my life look like if I cut ties with them and went to the man I believe I'm meant for?

I hear honking from outside. Long steady honks. Honks in the "Shave and a Haircut" rhythm. Then the song "Be My Baby."

I gasp and run to the front balcony.

"Dahlia! What are you doing?"

I ignore my mother's screech of horror behind me and step into the downpour. Throw myself against the railing to peer over.

Oh, God.

I cover my mouth to catch the sob.

He's there. Standing in the rain, leaning against a beautiful, cherry red convertible, staring up at me.

"Antonio!" I shout.

People are watching. Camera flashes go off. The paparazzi must be camped out, along with Antonio.

I see Bea there, too. She's climbing out of Antonio's car, like she was the one managing the music. She waves her arm in a giant arc.

Antonio spreads both hands. "Dahlia. Please come down."

I look over my shoulder. "I can't. There are guards at the door."

More flashbulbs go off. The press is getting every word of this.

I see the sudden danger in Antonio as his shoulders stiffen, and he pushes away from the car.

"No, wait!" I don't want any more bloodshed. Not on my account.

I throw one leg over the balcony railing.

"No, *Principessa!*" Antonio lunges into traffic, causing cars to screech to a halt as he bolts across the road.

"Catch me," I challenge. We're only three floors up. I know without a shadow of a doubt Antonio won't let me fall.

"No, no, no! Wait, Dahlia!"

I don't wait. I slip off the slick balcony, screaming and flailing at the swift plunge. Air rushes past me, the sidewalk rushes up to meet me.

I fall squarely in Antonio's arms. My weight knocks him to the ground, and we tangle on the wet cement.

His lips find my ear, his arms squeeze me so tight I can't breathe. "Dahlia... Dahlia. My wild, feisty bride. My love."

"Antonio. I'm sorry about *The Honeymoon.*"

Antonio gives a soft laugh, rolling me over to face him. Our clothes are soaked, and he's on his back in a puddle. "The yacht or our actual event?"

"I mean what happened." Tears fill my eyes. "I shouldn't have sent word to my father. "

He cradles my face and pulls my lips down to his. "No, no, no, *amore.* You did nothing wrong. I had no right to take you against your will. Forgive me."

I nod, tears spilling down my already wet cheeks. "I forgive you. Do you forgive me?"

"Nothing to forgive. You are perfect."

A crowd of people has gathered around us now. Flash-bulbs still go off.

Antonio lifts me off him to get to his feet and help me

stand. His hands coast over me, his gaze rakes over my body. "Are you hurt?"

I shake my head.

He extends a hand in the direction of his car across the street. "Your chariot awaits, my lady."

Someone bursts into applause nearby, cheering at the top of her lungs.

Bea.

I rush to her and give her a giant hug as the rest of the crowd break into applause and cheering.

"Ah, yes. I met your delightful bridesmaid again. She was a great help to me in finding the music to draw you out." He leans over to give Bea a cheek kiss.

"Come, my sweet wife." He sweeps me up into his arms. "Our future is waiting."

\* \* \*

*Antonio*

I carry my beautiful wife across the threshold of my penthouse. We're still wet from the rain, and her cheeks are flushed. Her big blue eyes are soft on my face, making me feel taller than the Empire State Building. She's been looking at me that way ever since I caught her under the balcony.

*Goddamn,* my heart stopped in that moment. I will have nightmares until the day I die. If she'd been hurt–if I hadn't caught her, or my body hadn't broken the fall–I never would have recovered.

She ignores the interior of my loft as I carry her through it and into the bathroom in the master suite. Instead, she's apparently fascinated, still, by my face. She's touching my jaw, pushing my wet hair out of my eyes.

I set her down in the bathroom and tug her wet blouse over her head then slide her pants and panties down her legs. She unhooks her bra and tosses it to the marble floor.

She unbuttons my shirt as I toe off my shoes, and then I find her mouth. I haven't kissed her properly since the day *The Honeymoon* sank at sea. Haven't claimed her sweet mouth or seen her naked. I haven't been able to touch or taste her skin.

I strip out of the rest of my clothes as I kiss her then walk her backward until we're under the spray.

"I missed my wife." My voice sounds rusty.

"I missed you, too." Dahlia picks up the bar of soap and strokes it across my chest.

I close my eyes, savoring the moment. Drinking it in. Celebrating what has become. This was not a future I ever foresaw. In fact, I don't think my revenge plan ever got past our I-do's at the altar.

It's so much sweeter than taking King Yachts. So much richer than having the last word with Benedict King.

It's far more magical, even than getting the girl I was told I wasn't worthy of.

This moment is real. It's now. Dahlia isn't some stuck-up debutante I want to bring to heel. She's the vibrant, talented, three-dimensional woman touching me, who, against all reason, has chosen my side. Has offered herself up to me–willingly, this time.

I open my eyes and take the soap from her. Rubbing it between my hands, I generate suds, then stroke around her breasts.

"I'm going to make you happy," I promise her.

She sways on her feet, her lids drooping.

"You can have anything you want. Voice lessons, performances, your own band. Whatever makes my wife smile, I will make it happen."

Her face lights up with a smile that slays me.

I go down on one knee to soap each leg, then stroke all around her ass and between her cheeks.

She doesn't giggle or squirm, she receives my intimate touch like she's the queen, and it's her due–which it is.

The tether on my self-control snaps, and I press her against the wall, lifting one of her legs over my shoulder to get at her core. I lick into her, pinning her pelvis to the tile, so I can properly pleasure her.

She grasps my head, first to steady herself then to pull me against her hot flesh, urging me on. I work her clit with my tongue as I slide my fingers along her cleft. She wants more though. She grasps my wrist and presses my fingers against her. I screw one in and slowly pump as I suck the nubbin of her clit.

"Yes," she moans. "Please, Antonio."

*Fanculo.* Her begging makes me lose all control. I add a second finger and pump. Her moan gets louder and louder and rises in pitch until it's almost a scream.

I can't take it anymore. I rise and turn her to face the tile wall. After spreading her legs, and pulling her hips back, I line up my cock with her entrance.

I try to go slowly. Try to remember she's practically still a virgin. But then she pushes that ass back at me, and I forget to be gentle. I grip her hips and shove into her, flattening her chest against the tile. Our two bodies meld as one, in a perfect rhythm and synchronicity. Her cries blend with my panting breath. Each forceful thrust brings us to the brink of ecstasy. We are glorying in the moment, this moment when we stopped becoming individuals and became one united force. Dahlia belongs to me, and I belong to her. We are everything together.

I don't know how long our love-making goes on. I know at one point I pull out, turn her around, and pin her against the wall the other way. I know her arms are twined around my neck, her throaty cries croon right in my ear. I know she's calling my name, and I'm calling hers. And it goes on and on, as if making up for our seven years apart, for our tumultuous beginnings. This is the way we affirm what we are now. Our marriage. Our union. Our truce.

This is the way I get the ultimate revenge fuck. The one that initiates an entirely new life, full of love, communion, and Dahlia.

# Epilogue

**D**ahlia

I'm beyond nervous. I run my hands down the midnight blue mini-dress that clings to my curves. A pair of matching thigh-high go-go boots complete the outfit. I'm about to go out on stage and sing. The trouble is, a planned performance is totally different than grabbing the mic while I'm drunk in Miami.

Antonio's uncle, Don Beretta, is hosting a private anniversary party for me and Antonio at one of his nightclubs, and Antonio asked me to sing a song as an anniversary present. I chose Peggy Lee's recent version of "Fever." It's sexy and sultry and speaks to the burning romance I have with my new husband.

What I didn't expect, though, was to see my parents escorted in and given the front-row seats beside Bea.

She looks as surprised as I feel, so I know she didn't invite them. I haven't spoken to them since the day I jumped off the balcony. That day, I became a part of Antonio's world and left high society life behind. I haven't missed it once.

Bea remains my steadfast friend (much to her parents' dismay), and I've been welcomed fully into the Beretta clan. I now have lively cousins and sisters and friends. The Berettas are a tight, loud, lively bunch.

Antonio must have orchestrated my parents' presence. I can't decide if I want to kiss him, slap him, or cry. Maybe I'll do all three. It's too late to back out of singing or curse at my husband now, though. The band leader is introducing me.

Eek!

My legs tremble as I step out on stage and take the microphone. The band is already playing the music to the song. We practiced this afternoon, and it went beautifully. There's no reason for me to panic. No reason other than I wanted to sing to Antonio and feel sexy and now my parents, who hate my singing and would find my open sexuality an affront to my upbringing, are here.

But screw them. This is my anniversary. This is my world. A year ago today my real life started. The life where I am myself, all of me, where I'm loved for who I am, not what I represent. Not how I reflect on another.

I look around for Antonio. This song is his gift, after all. I'm shocked to find he's taking the seat beside my mother. All three of them are now sitting around a small cocktail table in front of the stage.

My husband leans back in his chair, his dark glittering gaze on mine as he lights a cigar. He winks, and that's all I need for my power to return.

Because Antonio does make me feel powerful.

He makes me feel beautiful and talented and strong. And I haven't missed my old life for one moment. Yes, the rift between me and my parents has bothered me, but I haven't missed living under their control or the pressure to perform for them.

I keep my eyes glued to my husband's handsome face and sway my hips slowly to the music. The moment I begin to sing, I forget my nerves. I forget that my parents might disapprove. I stop worrying about why they're here or what I will say to them afterward. I just feel the music. Embody the music. Sing out of pure joy. Out of love. Out of total devotion to the man who is totally devoted to me.

Antonio's gaze never leaves my face, and it tells me everything: that he's as enamored as I am. As bewitched. As feverishly in love. It's strange, but our love only seems to grow.

By the time I finish the song, I realize that everyone's watching. Even Don Beretta and the Family men who were talking loudly amongst themselves when I began are quiet now, staring at me.

I complete the last note and fumble as I put the microphone back in the stand.

Did I embarrass them? Maybe the Berettas don't like me singing in public either.

A chance of glance at my parents, and I'm shocked to see a tear running down my mother's face. She climbs unsteadily to her feet. She's going to walk out now without even saying anything to me.

But no, she stands and begins clapping. She's giving me a standing ovation.

The smoky lounge erupts with applause. There's a roar of cheers. Some people call my name. Bea, I think. And Antonio.

It takes me a moment to recover, but a smile breaks out on my face, and I take a bow.

My dad stands up—although I think I saw Antonio give him the evil eye first.

I bow again, heat and pressure building in my chest and behind my face like I'm going to cry.

Instead of heading off stage, Antonio holds his hand out to me, and I jump down from the stage apron and fall against him. He envelopes me in a hug and kisses my forehead. "Bravo, *Principessa*. *Grazie*. I loved the song. You were incredible."

"You invited my parents," I croak.

"I did. It's time to mend fences, *amore*." He turns me toward my mother and nudges me forward.

My mom holds back. It's an awkward moment until Bea throws an arm around each of our shoulders and pulls us in for a group hug. "Wasn't she amazing, Mrs. King?"

My mom doesn't answer. It probably would be too much to concede in front of Bea, when my singing is an embarrassment. Instead, she bursts into tears.

"Oh, Dahlia! Are you okay? You look so happy. I missed you so much."

I pull my mom into a real hug and pat her back like she's the child and I'm the parent. "I missed you, too, Mom. I'm very happy with Antonio. I love him."

I sense Antonio's gaze on me when I say those words and turn to see him speaking to my father. He propels my father toward me, and I endure another awkward hug.

"Nice singing, honey. Beautiful dress."

Not really the words I need from my father, but it's a start.

Champagne is uncorked and someone wheels out a giant, tiered cake as if it's our wedding and not just our first anniversary.

"Cake is being served. You'll stay for cake, no?" Antonio asks my parents. "Sit down with Dahlia here. You three catch up. Bea, too–the four of you. I need to make the rounds."

My vision goes blurry for a moment at the thoughtfulness of my husband. The ease with which he moves mountains and orchestrates miracles.

God bless Bea, who starts talking brightly about the band and my dress and the weather.

"I love you." My father interrupts Bea's monologue.

We all stare at him in surprise. He's not the kind of man to express emotion. "I'm glad you're safe. I never would have forgiven myself if that–" He seems to bite his tongue against whatever name he was going to call Antonio. "–if your husband had been cruel to you. But it seems he loves you. And I guess that's all that matters in the end."

There's a look of defeat around my father that I don't like to see, but I remind myself that he made his own bed.

I lean over and kiss his cheek. "I love you, too, Daddy."

One of the servers slides cake and champagne in front of each of us and across the room, Antonio clinks his glass to bring the room to silence.

"I wish to toast my beautiful wife." He lifts his glass. "Eight years ago, I got a job on a yacht where I kissed the most beautiful girl in the world. It utterly changed the course of my life." There's a wryness to his tone, and the room rumbles the same wry sound back. Everyone here knows what happened next because there are no secrets in big Italian families. They know what my father did. The storm of vengeance Antonio became in response.

My mother-in-law glares at my father. She loves me, but she will never forgive him, even if Antonio has embraced the outcome of it all.

"No no." Antonio holds a hand out. "Let there be no disparagement of my father-in-law. He found me unworthy then, which caused me to make something of myself. And I have." Antonio spreads his arms wide and the room erupts in cheers. It's true. In the year that we've been married, I learned that Antonio basically runs the Beretta crime family now. The don is mostly retired. His nephew rose up faster through the ranks than any man ever has and took the helm along, generating hundreds of millions of dollars.

The yacht business, it turns out, was key to allowing the Berettas to move their weapons dealing across international waters with total ease. Antonio also made King Yachts profitable again, without any infusion of dirty money.

"And while I thought I was making myself into something powerful so that I could wield my revenge, it turns out, Mr King was right. I needed to make myself worthy of Dahlia. Because she is my everything. And I would do anything to keep her happy."

*Aw, damn.* My mascara is going to run. I dab at the corners of my eyes. Antonio finds my gaze and lifts his glass. "So this toast is to you, *Principessa.* My darling Dahlia. You're the love of my life."

"Awww." Some of the female guests sigh.

Antonio ignores them, going on. "Thank you for being my wife."

My mom holds a cloth napkin over her mouth to cover a sob.

I stand from the table and walk slowly across the room with my gaze fixed on my husband's handsome face. It's like it's our wedding day–a real wedding day–and I'm walking down the aisle to meet him. To seal our futures together forever.

He sets down his glass when he sees me coming and takes both my hands in his. "Marry me?" he asks. I laugh-sob and nod, the tears escaping my eyes for real now.

"I love you, Mrs. Beretta."

"I love you."

The crowd cheers.

"*Saluti*," calls Don Beretta and everyone lifts their glass and drinks. Everyone except for me and Antonio because we're locked in a bone-melting kiss

"Come here." He takes my hand, and we slip out of the room as the party-goers turn to their cake and champagne.

Antonio pulls me into a back office where he slips an envelope out of his inner coat pocket and hands it to me. "This is my present to you."

"What is it?"

"Go on." He nods toward the envelope. "Open it."

I don't know why my fingers tremble as I open it. I know it's not something unwanted, like divorce papers. It's just the emotion of the moment, I guess. The overwhelm of being loved this thoroughly and well.

I unfold the sheaf of papers and start to skim. They *are* legal papers.

"You're signing King Yachts over to me?"

"Yes. It's up to you if you want to return it to your father. He's been reaping the benefits of it anyway, as I've paid his salary for the last year."

"You...you have? You've been paying my father's salary." I can't keep the disbelief from my voice. "Has he been working for you?"

Antonio gives a dry laugh. "No. Nor do I want him to. But I couldn't let your parents starve."

I let out a watery laugh. "They wouldn't have starved. They could have sold off half their properties and lived on the interest from the proceeds for the rest of their lives."

"Well, I didn't want them to suffer. They're your parents. That means they're my family too."

This man. He may be a cut-throat businessman, but underneath it all, he's a big softie.

"I'm not returning it to my father. This is a legitimate business, and we're keeping it for our family. Our future children. It will be our legacy."

Antonio cradles my face. "I can't wait to begin that family, *Principessa*."

And now for my real anniversary present–far better than a song at a party. Something that will last a lifetime.

I beam up at him. "We already have."

# Excerpt from DEN OF SINS

*Hannah*

This can't be happening. Is this really happening?

Is there a bloody man lying dead in the middle of my florist shop?

The room is silent but for the sound of a ticking clock and the ringing in my ears.

Armando curses and drops to his knees, checking the guy's pulse.

Then he moves quickly—all efficiency and practice. He locks my door, closes the blinds and turns the sign to closed. He picks up the gun then drags the body past the counter toward the back. "Don't move," he tells me as he passes.

*Don't move.*

I don't know why, but until that moment, I hadn't considered *my* life might be in danger.

I was an observer, and I was rooting for one side to win.

My pick won the round.

But now it sets in that we're not going to be slapping high fives here. A guy *just got killed* in my shop, and I witnessed it.

I'm the *only* witness.

And the killer told me not to move. Which means I should definitely move.

Armando drags the body into my cooler. He's going to come out here and deal with me next.

That's a problem. I grab my purse and quietly, quickly walk past the cooler.

I sense Armando near, but I don't stop. I know if I do, it will be my last mistake. My heart pounds, and I can feel the sweat on my palms. I'm almost halfway to freedom when I hear a noise from the back of the shop. I spin to see Armando walking slowly towards me, gun in hand and a menacing look on his face. He's not going to let me go this easily. He takes a few more steps towards me, and I know I'm not going to make it out alive. I turn back towards the door, but it's too late. He's almost at me now, and there's no escape.

"Stop. I said don't fucking move!" That voice. He does command so well, every cell in my body wants to obey.

But that would be stupid, so I break into a run.

*"Hannah."*

Surprise that he remembered my name makes me falter. The hesitation costs me. He's on me in a flash, grabbing my elbow and whipping me around.

"I said, *don't move.*"

God, he's still devastatingly handsome. Square jaw. Aquiline nose. Hazel eyes with long lashes. He's so close, I smell the scent of Rocco's shaving cream on him. He's in a crisp, expensive blue button-down, open at the throat to reveal a clean white undershirt.

"I'm on your side," I say on exhale.

I'm not sure if it's self-preservation that makes me say

the words or if it's the actual truth. I know Armando. I actually always liked the man... maybe a little too much.

I am on his side. I am.

He pivots me to face the wall, tugging one of my hands to pin there.

"I told you not to move." This is the voice of a mad man. Of the mafia. A killer. I need to remember that.

"I'm not going to say a thing." The famous last words of people before they are killed.

This is it. I'm dead.

# Den of Sins

**She's my captive. A witness to my crime. I'll never let her go.**

I'm a desperate man. One week out of prison
  and trouble found me again. When a mafia hitman comes after me,
  I end him with my bare hands. But the beautiful florist witnesses my crime.
  Now she's my prisoner. I can't let her go.
  My soul's unsalvageable, forever living in a den of sin.
  But the rest of me knows what it wants.
  And I want her.

Read DEN OF SINS

# Want FREE books?

# Other Titles by Renee Rose

*Alpha's Vow*

*Alpha's Revenge*

*Alpha's Fire*

*Alpha's Rescue*

*Alpha's Command*

## Werewolves of Wall Street

*Big Bad Boss: Midnight*

*Big Bad Boss: Moon Mad*

Big Bad Boss: Marked

Big Bad Boss: Mated

## Alpha Doms Series

*The Alpha's Hunger*

*The Alpha's Promise*

*The Alpha's Punishment*

*The Alpha's Protection (Dirty Daddies)*

## Two Marks Series

*Untamed*

*Tempted*

*Desired*

*Enticed*

## Wolf Ranch Series

*Rough*

*Wild*

*Feral*

*Savage*

*Fierce*

*Ruthless*

## Contemporary

## Chicago Sin

*Den of Sins*

*Rooted in Sin*

## Made Men Series

*Don't Tease Me*

*Don't Tempt Me*

*Don't Make Me*

## Chicago Bratva

*"Prelude" in Black Light: Roulette War*

*The Director*

*The Fixer*

*"Owned" in Black Light: Roulette Rematch*

*The Enforcer*

*The Soldier*

*The Hacker*

*The Bookie*

*The Cleaner*

*The Player*

*The Gatekeeper*

## Alpha Mountain

*Hero*

*Rebel*

*Warrior*

**Vegas Underground Mafia Romance**

*King of Diamonds*

*Mafia Daddy*

*Jack of Spades*

*Ace of Hearts*

*Joker's Wild*

*His Queen of Clubs*

*Dead Man's Hand*

*Wild Card*

**Daddy Rules Series**

*Fire Daddy*

*Hollywood Daddy*

*Stepbrother Daddy*

***Master Me Series***

*Her Royal Master*

*Her Russian Master*

*Her Marine Master*

*Yes, Doctor*

***Double Doms Series***

*Theirs to Punish*

*Theirs to Protect*

***Holiday Feel-Good***

*Scoring with Santa*

*Saved*

## Other Contemporary

*Black Light: Valentine Roulette*

*Black Light: Roulette Redux*

*Black Light: Celebrity Roulette*

*Black Light: Roulette War*

*Black Light: Roulette Rematch*

*Punishing Portia (written as Darling Adams)*

*The Professor's Girl*

*Safe in his Arms*

## Sci-Fi

## Zandian Masters Series

*His Human Slave*

*His Human Prisoner*

*Training His Human*

*His Human Rebel*

*His Human Vessel*

*His Mate and Master*

*Zandian Pet*

*Their Zandian Mate*

*His Human Possession*

## Zandian Brides

*Night of the Zandians*

*Bought by the Zandians*

*Mastered by the Zandians*

*Zandian Lights*

*Kept by the Zandian*

*Claimed by the Zandian*

*Stolen by the Zandian*

*Rescued by the Zandian*

## Other Sci-Fi

*The Hand of Vengeance*

*Her Alien Masters*

# About Renee Rose

**USA TODAY BESTSELLING AUTHOR RENEE ROSE** loves a dominant, dirty-talking alpha hero! She's sold over two million copies of steamy romance with varying levels of kink. Her books have been featured in USA Today's *Happily Ever After* and *Popsugar*. Named Eroticon USA's Next Top Erotic Author in 2013, she has also won *Spunky and Sassy's* Favorite Sci-Fi and Anthology author, *The Romance Reviews* Best Historical Romance, and has hit the *USA Today* list fifteen times with her Bad Boy Alphas, Chicago Bratva, and Wolf Ranch series.

*Renee loves to connect with readers!*
www.reneeroseromance.com
reneeroseauthor@gmail.com

facebook.com/reneeroseromance
instagram.com/reneeroseromance
bookbub.com/authors/renee-rose